THE
SAN SEBASTIAN

EILÍS DILLON

THE
SAN SEBASTIAN

First published 1953 by Faber and Faber Ltd
Paperback edition published 1980 by
The Hamlyn Publishing Group Ltd

This edition published 1996
by Poolbeg Press Ltd
123 Baldoyle Industrial Estate
Dublin 13, Ireland

© Eilís Dillon 1953

The moral right of the author has been asserted.

The Publishers gratefully acknowledge the support of
The Arts Council.

A catalogue record for this book is available from the British Library.

ISBN 1 85371 666 9

Cover illustration by Marie Louise Fitzpatrick
Cover design by Poolbeg Group Services Ltd
Set by Poolbeg Group Services Ltd in Garamond 11/14
Printed by The Guernsey Press Ltd,
Vale, Guernsey, Channel Islands.

About the Author

Eilís Dillon was born in Galway. She was one of Ireland's leading writers, having published many children's and adult novels, as well as poetry, plays and short stories. Eilís Dillon died in 1994.

Also by Eilís Dillon

The Coriander
The Sea Wall
The Singing Cave
The Lion Cub

Praise for *The Sea Wall*

"Eilís Dillon shows great insight into the strengths and weaknesses of human nature."
The Examiner

" . . . A great storyteller . . . "
The Examiner

For Cormac Og

Contents

1	I Discover the Brig	1
2	The Coming of Manuel	18
3	The Face at the Window	36
4	Eric	56
5	Manuel Departs	70
6	I Set Out for Galway	88
7	Juan	105
8	The House in the Rocks	126
9	The Whalers' Island	139
10	News of the *San Sebastian*	159
11	We Start for Home	176
12	The *San Sebastian* Sails Again	191
13	The Battle	211
14	The End of the Story	226

1

I Discover the Brig

As long as I live I shall never forget the morning I looked out and saw the *San Sebastian* floating quietly under my window. It was a morning of early summer and the sea was calm and silvery, with no sign now of the storm of the night before. I had woken several times during the night to hear the waves thundering on the shore, and the wild wind neighing around the house. It was only on nights like this that I wished I did not live alone.

The whitewashed cottage in which my ancestors had lived for hundreds of years was perched on a height above the Connemara shore. It faced west, full into the Atlantic gales, so that my front door had to stay firmly shut for half the year. The back was sheltered from the mean east wind by the two-peaked mountain that we called the Minaun, which means a kid-goat. The peaks looked just like budding horns. Rocky fields stretched away behind the house, and a rough boreen twisted its way between them to the road that ran at the foot of the mountain. I owned nearly thirty acres of those fields, but they were so poor that it took endless labour to get a living from them. Without the help of my neighbour, Bartley Folan, I could not have managed at all.

Bartley was surely the best neighbour that ever anyone had. When my father, whose name was Pat Hernon like my own, was lost with his currach a year ago, many people had said that a boy of fourteen should not live alone. They said that I should sell the farm for what it would fetch and apprentice myself to a trade in Galway. The idea of doing this filled me with horror. I could not endure the prospect of living away from the sea. The sea comes into Galway, to be sure, but it is a tamed sea, closed into the bay, fit only for the summer people to dabble their toes in. I explained this to Bartley as best I could, and after he had thought it over for a day or two he told the people that they could be quite easy about my future, that he was going to look after me himself. His own family was grown up long since, and all gone to America, and it would be like old times, he said, to have a boy about the place.

I soon found that, though I could never forget my own father, Bartley had gradually begun to take his place. Because he had always had to work too hard, Bartley looked older than his sixty years. His shoulders were bent and his hair was snow-white. But for all that he was an expert at farming our

2

unwilling land, and it was a joy to watch him handle a boat. We often went fishing together, usually in Bartley's currach, though I had one of my own, too. Bartley had helped me to make it, to replace the one that had disappeared with my father. He showed me how to stretch canvas over a wooden frame, and tar the canvas to make it waterproof.

I continued to sleep in my own house, but every day I went to Bartley's cottage, a few fields away, for dinner. I spent the winter evenings there, too, sitting at the fire, while Mrs Folan knitted socks or worked her spinning-wheel. Bartley's house was a favourite gathering-place for the people from the scattered farms and cottages of the district. On any evening one might find Lazy Johnny O'Neill there, who was called Lazy Johnny to distinguish him from Johnny O'Neill from Casla, as hard-working a man as you could hope to find. Then there was the tailor, Michael Conneeley, but no one ever called him anything except Tailor. He made suits for the whole neighbourhood, suits of strong glasheen-caorach, cut to a special pattern, decent on Sunday for five years and fit for every-day use for ten years after that. There was Ned Donnelly, the blacksmith and wheelwright, and little Joe Fahy, the weaver. All these lived in Farran, the village by our quay, and better than anything else they loved talk and news and problems to be settled and questions to be solved. I was remembering this and their burning curiosity as I jumped into my clothes as fast as I could that morning while the *San Sebastian* floated serenely in the sea below my window.

My old clock had stopped, but I knew by the sun that it was very early. There was a good chance that no one was awake but myself. I hurried outside, and I remember how I paused for a second to admire the ship in the clear morning light. What a little beauty she was! Often after a storm we used to find wrack washed up on this part of the coast. Sometimes very strange things had come in, but I had never before seen a whole ship waiting to be picked up. I felt a sudden wild longing to own her, so that I could sail her up and down the world as long as we both lived. I had a good chance of owning her, I knew, for we had a tradition that whoever saves a piece of wreck has a right to it afterwards. But as to sailing her, that was another story.

I guessed that she was of the brigantine class, from the descriptions I had heard in the old men's stories. She had no sail up now, but I could see that she was square-rigged. Her sails had been untidily stowed by someone in a hurry. She was some sixty feet long, and seemed to be built of strong, dark wood. Although she was very old, she gave an impression of being well cared for, perhaps because of the polished brasses on the deck, glinting in the sun. I guessed that she was deserted, because of the way she swung with the tide, while her rudder creaked.

With my heart pounding, I leaped down to the

shore over the rocks. My feet were bare, so that I could move like a goat for speed. My currach was there, safe in a sheltered place out of reach of the sea. It was no easy job to carry it down and launch it single-handed, without tearing the canvas, but I had done this before, and though I had to be slow and cautious at last I had it afloat. I hopped in and began to row towards the brig.

Where could she have come from? I could almost have believed that she was the famous enchanted barque of Manannan, waiting to lure sailors to destruction. She certainly looked out of place in Connemara, where the sailing boats were tough, black, tarry hookers with brown sails, and with the smell of turf and fish ingrained in them. She was as delicate as a well-tempered sword, and like a good sword, her designer had had a care for her looks. It broke my heart to think of the danger she was in, for I knew that if I could not tow her to safety she would drift in on to the rocks along the coast and be smashed to pieces. I was not deceived by the calm of the sea. At this time of the year it could not remain calm for long and even now the small waves struck on the shingle with a wicked little crash.

Glancing over my shoulder now and then, I made the currach fly over the water. At last I lifted my oars and drifted in within a few feet of the little ship. Now for the first time I was able to read her name, the *San Sebastian,* carved on her bows and painted in gold. I looked up at the magnificent figurehead above me. It was the head of a young man, Saint Sebastian, I supposed, carved in wood and painted in dark colours. With lifted chin and fierce, proud gaze, he stared forever along the course his ship would follow. I had once or twice seen figureheads on Norwegian ships in the docks at Galway, but compared with this they were tame and lifeless.

The currach bumped softly against the ship's side. I eased myself along with my hands on the sun-warmed wood, along the whole length of her, across her stern and around to the other side. She looked very tall from the level of the sea, so that I wondered how I would be able to climb aboard. Then I saw a rope ladder dangling over the side ahead of me.

It was a new ladder, of clean white rope, strongly made. In a moment I had tied the old painter of my currach to it and was climbing on board. I swung my legs over the wooden rail and dropped on to the deck.

The brig was about sixty feet long, as I had guessed. Her foremast was quite short, not much bigger than the mast of a hooker, but she had a tall mainmast, which was obviously meant to carry topsails. Near me where I stood in the bows there was an open hatch, with a companionway just visible leading downwards. Towards the stern there were cabins on deck, with a wheel-house before them. Walking very softly I went into the wheel-house. There was so little way on the brig that she would not respond properly when I swung the wheel, but lurched uneasily until I let go.

Leaving the wheel-house, I thought I would next examine the cabins. I stepped over the high, brassbound threshold and into a little passageway. Five doors opened off it, two on either side and one at the end. They were not locked, and I went into each cabin in turn. Everything I saw filled me with delight. The first three were fitted with bunks and shelves with brass rails. Each had a lamp swinging from the ceiling. They were all panelled in the same warm, dark wood, and they all had the same sweet smell of well-polished wood and brass. There were some books on the shelves, bound in soft old leather, but when I opened one or two, I found that I could not understand them, for they were written in a strange language.

The fourth cabin was the biggest, and I guessed that it had been the Captain's cabin, and perhaps the officers' dining-room as well. It had a polished round table and several bracket lamps, as well as a central swinging lamp. Through the portholes I could see my own house, framed as if it were a little picture, and seeming to swing gently up and down with the motion of the brig. Under the portholes there was a bureau with drawers and a flat top, to be used as a writing desk. There were leather-padded benches against the other walls. It was all perfectly clean, and there was no sign that it had been recently used.

I went out into the passageway again and opened the end door, and here at last I found signs of human occupation. I was in a little galley, so small that there

was only room for me to stand up. There was a
primus stove, on a sheet of tin for safety, and an
empty can which seemed to have contained beans.
There was a saucepan there, too, in which the beans
had been heated, and a very old iron spoon which
someone had used to eat them with. Not a tidy eater,
I thought, as I observed the splashed shelf and floor.
And then I remembered the storm, and wondered if it
had interrupted the bean-eater's meal. It looked as if
there had only been one man on board when the
storm broke, unless they had taken turns with the
spoon. But then I remembered that I had not
explored the whole of the brig yet, and I left the
galley by another door and came out on deck. I had
absent-mindedly carried the empty bean-tin with me,
and now, before I turned towards the bows, I sent
the tin flying through the air in the direction of the
shore. It landed right side up, and I could see it
bobbing gently up and down.

At the top of the companionway I paused. It was
dim down there, and I would be quite helpless as I
descended step by step. Anyone lurking there would
have me by the leg before I could make a move to
save myself. I went to the side to be sure my currach
was safe, and was reassured to see it exactly as I had
left it, drifting along gently with the brig. I noticed
too, that though I could hardly feel any movement,
we were travelling along the line of the shore so that
my cottage was no longer directly above. We were
off the low black cliffs now, and soon we would

sight Bartley's house. There was no time to fear for my own skin. And after all, I came as a rescuer, and if there was anyone on the brig, he should feel grateful to me instead of attacking me.

I walked a few cautious steps down the companion ladder, and then dropped on to the deck below. The light was poor here, coming from a ring of portholes around the bows of the ship. I held my breath for a moment and listened. There was no sound, except for the gentle slap of the sea against the ship's sides. I peered about for a moment, until I became accustomed to the dimness. Then I could see even into the farthest corners. There was no one there.

I supposed that this part of the ship would be called the forecastle, and was meant for the use of the crew. It covered the full width of the ship, and about one quarter of her length. I thought that there must be a big hold stretching from here to the stern below decks. In such a little ship there was not likely to be a lower deck. There were bunks around the walls, with old brown blankets folded on four of them. There were hooks for swinging hammocks too, but no hammocks. A table of rough wood was screwed to the middle of the deck, but though it was rough it had been well polished. The white planks of the deck had been scrubbed clean, but there was a ring of dirty boot-marks around the table.

I was becoming more and more bewildered by each of my discoveries. It was plain that she was an old ship, so old that I guessed that all her sister ships were broken up this many a year. And yet she was sea-worthy, else, how could be have weathered last night's storm, which must have sent the hookers home like a flock of crows, and the trawlers scurrying for the shelter of the Aran Islands? Then, judging by the blankets on the bunks, she seemed to have had several men on her at one time, but why had they not navigated her safely through the storm? Had they become frightened and taken to the boats? I had noticed that one lifeboat was missing. And what about the tin of beans, which seem to show that there had been only one man on board when the storm broke? I could believe that while one man could manage the brig for a time in good weather, he would be quite helpless in a storm. And where was this man now? Gone overboard, perhaps, or washed out of his lifeboat by a wave and drowned. If this had happened I could expect to see the lifeboat coming along presently, for it was likely enough to follow the currents that had sent the brig to me.

I ran up on deck again and looked about me. The village was still asleep, with not the smallest feather of smoke to be seen. Beyond it, away to the east, a long reef of rocks hid my view of the open sea. I guessed that the brig had come in from the north-west, made a wide half-circle off the point of the reef and turned west again along by the shore. This was the way that heavy wrack usually behaved, as I had often observed. Bartley and I used to watch it from the top of the little cliffs, and when it would have rounded the reef, we would run for the currach and row out to capture it. In this way we had brought in bales of wood and sacks of meal and many other useful things. If we failed to reach it in time or if the sea was too rough, the wrack was usually thrown on to the big black rocks beyond Bartley's house and smashed about until it was useless. This was what I feared would happen to the *San Sebastian* if I could not get her to safety in time.

Back in the captain's cabin I tried the drawers of the bureau one by one. They were all unlocked and empty except one, and this I prised open with my pocket knife. I hated to injure the wood, but there was no help for it. A piece broke away in my hand, and it looked like earthenware, it was so old and dry. I pulled the drawer open, and there was what I sought, a little pile of papers. I looked through them quickly. They were real parchment, though I did not know this at the time, and they were handwritten in the same strange language that I had seen in the books on the shelves. I did not know then that it was Spanish, though I have since come to know and love that language as if I had been born to the sound of it. As I fingered the sheets I was thinking that these must be what are called the ship's "papers" of which I had often heard, and which I knew would prove that it was I who had saved her from wreck if anyone ever doubted my word. I buttoned them safely into the inside pocket of my jacket, pushed the drawer shut and went out on deck again.

In the bows I found what I wanted, a stout steel hawser, coiled under a rail, and obviously meant to be tied to a bollard when the ship was in dock. This was a thing that puzzled me, even while I thanked my stars for it: though the furnishings of the ship were all of a great age, the rope ladder and this hawser were quite new. I could not see properly against the sun, but I thought that the rigging had also been carefully renewed. I planned to spend many an hour examining her at my leisure, when I would have her in a place of safety.

I knew exactly where I wanted to take her. Beyond the black rocks the cliffs rose again to some sixty feet above sea level. And in the cliff face, to be reached only from the sea, there was a long high cave. Even at low tide there was always a good depth of water inside, and I thought that if I could get the brig in there she would be as snug as if she were in dock. I guessed that the cave would just hold her, for it ran a great distance under the cliff. It was not dark, for there were several holes in the roof. In winter, when the long waves raced through the cave, the spray shot up through these holes in a great plume. The people called them the Puffing-Holes. The land on the cliff-top belonged to Bartley, but it was not much use, being too salty and cold for crops and too dangerous for grazing animals.

I did not imagine that the local people would not

12

MS Connell

know that I had a brig hidden in the cave. If it had been a plank of wood they would have known within an hour. But I knew that they would respect my ownership, and they would never tell an outsider. If anyone were to come looking for the brig, he would be blandly questioned about his own affairs, and perhaps advised to visit me as a kind of afterthought, with the remark that I was a likely wideawake lad, who might be expected to notice anything strange that floated by. Then I would be left to handle the affair in my own way. I felt in my bones that someone would come to ask about the fate of the *San Sebastian.* I could not imagine such a prize being abandoned without protest, unless all her crew was drowned.

I took the end of the steel hawser and tied it around my middle. I climbed down the rope ladder and dropped into my currach, and fixed the hawser to a big hook in the stern. In a moment I had cast off and was rowing around to the bows of the brig. The hawser unrolled gradually and at last it was taut. I pulled steadily on my oars and watched the brig closely to see if she would respond. At first nothing happened, and I began to think she was going to prove too heavy for me. But then I felt a long drag, and she seemed to quicken her pace a little. She was no longer drifting. She was following my currach like a good dog following his master. My guess had been right. She was only a wooden ship, after all, and her balance was perfect. I had once seen two currachs

13

tow in a big English trawler which must have weighed twice as much.

I had only had time for a minute of this exultation before I became aware that something was wrong. The *San Sebastian* had followed me slowly for a few yards, to be sure, but now she seemed to be pulling against me, and her bows had turned a little seaward. I saw at once what had happened. The hawser came over the shore side, and therefore I was slowly pulling her stern about, until presently she would be broadside on to the direction I wanted her to take. It seemed that unless I could get the hawser to come exactly over the point of the bows I would not be able to manage her at all. And this would not be possible because the bowsprit would be in the way. It looked as if I was going to lose the brig altogether.

Just then I heard a faint shout from the shore. I was below Bartley's house now, and when I looked up I could see him running towards the shore, putting on his jacket as he ran. At the cottage door, Mrs Folan was standing with her head thrown back and her hands raised, and while I watched she doubled forward and straightened again. I did not have to hear any sound to know that she was helpless with laughter. It occurred to me for the first time that I must be a funny sight, trying to tow in a whole ship by myself. The thought made me grit my teeth and pull on the oars with all my might. I swore that if the *San Sebastian* would not follow me, I

14

would follow her wherever she might please to go. Lose her I would not.

Now Bartley had reached the shore. He waved to me and shouted again. He was making for his currach, and a moment later his voice floated out to me:

"Hold on to her, Pat! I'm coming!"

So it seemed I was not going to have the glory of rescuing her alone. I felt a little ashamed of myself now, for not having run over to Bartley's house and roused him to come with me. I had thought of nothing but of getting out to the brig as soon as possible. I waved and shouted back:

"All right, Bartley! We'll wait for you!"

He got his currach afloat and came skimming across the water to me. It seemed only a minute until he was beside me, one weatherbeaten hand grasping the gunwale of my currach and his face upturned in wonder at the brig's figurehead.

"Glory be to God!" he said at last. "This is the strangest sight I ever laid eyes on. Pat, where did she come from?"

"I don't know," said I. "I just looked out of the window and there she was. I've been all over her. There's no one aboard. I have her papers here."

I tapped the breast of my jacket.

"Good boy, good boy. What's her name?"

He peered at the name, but he was too short-sighted to read it at this distance.

"San Sebastian," said I. "I suppose that's himself

up there, looking over our heads. Oh, Bartley, she's a wonder to the world! Wait till you see her – cabins like a king's palace, and polish and shining brass everywhere. She was someone's pet ship, for certain."

"I'll believe that," said Bartley. "She must be a queer age. I never saw the like of her." He looked at me sharply. "Where are you trying to take her? To the cave below Puffing Holes, I suppose?" I nodded. "Yes, that's a good place, where inquisitive people won't find her. You were in trouble, I think, when I came along?"

"She was too big for me," I admitted. "It will take the two of us to get her into the cave."

"Two of us will not be enough," said Bartley. "I told herself to send a couple of the boys down to the cave to give us a hand. "Now don't be too independent," he said as he saw my expression. "She's your boat now. She was deserted when you found her. If we don't bring her in she'll be smashed up on the rocks for certain sure. So she's yours by the law of salvage. If the boys get a few evenings' talk and a fill of tobacco they will be quite satisfied."

"The boys" were all old men of Bartley's own age, but because they were bachelors they would be called boys till the day they died. I agreed that we would need help in getting her into the cave.

"If we can't get her to the cave mouth with the currachs," Bartley went on, "we can get out the lifeboat and tow her in. Now the first thing is to get another tow-line off the other side."

I was on board again in a moment, and had found and dropped him another hawser. Now we had one on either side of the bows, and when we tried them out we found that she followed the two currachs perfectly, along the line of the shore.

It was slow work, and by the time we reached the high cliffs we could see an excited group in currachs ahead of us at the mouth of the cave. A cheer went up from them as we came near, and then we could hear the men excitedly talking, admiring the brig and wondering at her strangeness.

I soon saw that without all these helpers we would have had no chance of getting her into the cave. They towed her and pushed her and turned her and steered her so that she sailed into the cave like a horse moving between the shafts of a cart. She had not much more room to spare than the horse would have had, on either side, but she was all inside the cave, and no one passing by on the sea would have guessed that she was there. We took one of the hawsers that we had used as a tow-rope, and looped it around a big rock at the back of the cave, and everyone agreed that she would be safe enough unless a real storm blew up. Then the men had to explore every inch of her, and lie on the bunks and sit at the tables, and wonder at length how she had managed to weather last night's storm.

Between everything, it was high noon by the time we left her and rowed back to the shore below Bartley's cottage.

2

The Coming of Manuel

I was ravenously hungry by now, for I had had no breakfast. Mrs Folan saw us coming, and she had a pot of strong red tea and a cartwheel of soda-bread on the table before us. While we ate she made us tell her all about the brig, and I had to promise to bring her around in the currach with me that very afternoon. This was an easy promise to make, for I was already longing to visit her again myself.

Some of the men had come in with us, and they had tea and soda-bread too. Soon they were speculating about the ownership of the brig. Lazy Johnny O'Neill was there, and he had been a most useful helper. He was never lazy when there was a bit of fun going on.

"Someone will come looking for that ship, you may be sure," he said. "It's a good thing we hid her, for if we left her at they quay they could just come along and sail her away without a word of thanks or any talk of salvage rights."

18

Bartley got his pipe going before he answered.

"We won't wait until someone comes. As soon as we can get a message into Galway, we'll ask Michael Daly what we should do."

Mr Daly was a solicitor, and a great friend of Bartley. The men nodded approval of this plan, and the tailor said it was a fine thing to have a friend like Mr Daly who knew everything and who was so obliging about giving advice.

"San Sebastian," said Joe Fahy, the weaver. "That sounds like a Spanish ship. What do you say, Tailor?"

"A Spanish ship, for sure," said the tailor, "or maybe a South American one. But if she was after coming from South America she'd be stuck all over with barnacles and seaweed, and there would be salt like snow caked all over her. Anyway I'd say she'd never weather a long voyage like that at this hour of her life, though she might have done it when she was younger."

They talked all around the story for an hour or more, and then they got up regretfully to go back to their work. Bartley got up too and went to the door with them. There was no need to ask them not to tell the news to strangers. As each man settled his cap on his head and walked away, he tightened his mouth and quenched the light of excitement in his eyes, lest it betray him.

When the last man was gone, Bartley turned to me and said urgently:

"Now Pat! The papers!"

I took the roll out of my pocket, and we laid them on the table. Mrs Folan came over too, and peered at them with us, but there were only three words that we recognised, repeated at intervals, and these were "San Sebastian" and "Valparaiso." At last Bartley straightened his back and said:

"Michael Daly will understand them, I'm sure, or he will find someone who will. You must keep them very carefully, Pat."

"I'm keeping them," announced Mrs Folan. "There's no one alive will succeed in getting them from me, you may go bail."

"That will be much better," said Bartley. "They will be safer here."

This arrangement pleased me very much. Mrs. Folan was about the same age as Bartley. With her soft white hair and gentle expression, she looked like a sweet, innocent countrywoman. But I knew she had the heart of a lion, and the decision and courage of a general on the battlefield. I rolled up the papers again and handed them to her without a word. I did not even ask her where she was going to hide them.

I had left my currach on the shore below Bartley's house, so instead of crossing the fields to go home, I went down to the sea. Bartley came with me to help launch the currach, and presently I was pulling slowly homewards with my head full of the morning's adventures. It was a wonder that I did not run myself on the rocks, for I was all in a dream with amazement at what had happened.

But when I reached my usual landing-place I came to myself with a jerk. There, knocking against the rocks by the side of my little beach, was a ship's lifeboat. I recognised it at once as having belonged to the *San Sebastian,* because the wood was the same. When I came closer I saw the name painted in the same gold letters on the bows. I was very pleased with myself for having guessed that the missing lifeboat would appear presently, and glad too that I had an excuse so soon for visiting the brig again. For of course, this tell-tale boat must be hidden as carefully as its mother.

I had a strong fishing-line on the floor of the currach and I thought I would be able to tow it with that. I pulled over to the lifeboat to attach my line, and then I stopped with the breath knocked out of me and my mouth open.

Lying in the boat, slumped forward, there was a man. He lay so low that I had not seen him until I came close. Whether he was alive or dead I did not know. He lay still enough for death. His broad black hat had fallen off, and the purple silk lining showed. His neck was darkly sunburned and his hair an oily black. He wore a suit of dark-blue cotton which would have left him shivering with the cold if he lived in the Irish climate. This and the sunburn and the broad-brimmed hat made me come to the conclusion at one glance that he was a foreigner, and that his own country was sunny and warm.

While these thoughts flashed through my mind, I

had hopped out on to the rocks, trusting my currach to mind itself. I gripped the side of the lifeboat and pulled it towards me. There were no oars in it. I eased it along by the rocks until I had it in shallow water, and then I jumped into the water beside it. In a moment I had it beached. I left it and returned for the currach, which I rowed in alongside the lifeboat. The tide was on the turn now, so I left the currach half in, half out of the water and turned my attention to the lifeboat.

For a moment I stood there, looking down at the man and reluctant to touch him. I shook his shoulder gently in case he had fallen into an exhausted sleep, but he did not move. I lifted him by the shoulders then, and laid him on his back, so that I could get my hand inside his shirt. Very faintly, I could feel his heart beating under my fingers, but he was miserably cold. The first thing was to get him near a fire. He was not a big man, but I knew he would be too heavy for me, and I wished Bartley had come with me.

Just then my old donkey, Simon, who had been on pension for several years, came to the grassy edge of the shore for the salty bite he liked so much.

"Hi Simon!" I called out to him. "Come along down here and do a bit of work for once!"

Fortunately donkeys do not understand English as well as they think they do, or Simon might have taken to his heels. Instead he picked his way delicately down to me, to see what I was at, and before he knew what was happening I had him by the mane. He gave me a very reproachful look, as only donkeys can, but he stood there meekly enough. It was well that he did, for it took time to get the stranger lying face downwards across his back. At last it was done, and with one hand on Simon's neck and the other holding the stranger so that he would not fall off, we started up the beach to my house.

At the top of the beach there was a rough road of big stones and sea sand, and a grassy lane led off this to my back door. I led Simon right into the kitchen, and made him wait while I pulled out the settle-bed by the fire. Then I got the stranger down off his back and into the bed as best I could. He landed with a thump, which I hoped would do him no harm, but there was no help for it. Then I turned Simon out, with a resounding wallop for thanks, and set to making a fire.

The fire had gone to sleep under a soft bed of ashes, but I raked it out and put on fresh turf, and presently I was fanning a little flame with my cap. All this time the stranger did not move, that I could see. Under the sunburn his face was as pale as a wax candle in the church. At last I was able to lift out a glowing sod of turf, break it up with the tongs and place a little saucepan of milk on it to heat. While I watched it I tried to control my patience. There was a strong temptation to let the man wait for a while and go down and hide the boat. But I could not take the risk of having him wake up while I was gone, and perhaps be bewildered by his surroundings.

Suddenly the doorway darkened and then Bartley came into the house saying:

"I thought of another thing, Pat – "

He stopped in astonishment as he caught sight of the stranger. He glanced sharply from him to the saucepan of milk, and understood the situation at once.

"Off the brig, of course," he said softly. "Where did you find him?"

"Washed up below there, in the missing lifeboat."

"How did you get him here?"

"On Simon's back."

"Wasn't he too heavy?"

"Heavy enough, but Simon is not as weak with age as he would like you to think."

"Is the lifeboat below still?"

"Yes. I was going to put it with the brig when I would have the man back in his senses again."

"That might be a day or maybe more. I'll put away the boat."

I reminded him to bring Mrs Folan with him to look at the brig, for it was clear that I was not going to be able to keep my promise to her. He left me then, as quickly as he had come, saying he would return as soon as he would have the lifeboat safe. I looked anxiously at the man, but he seemed not to have moved.

Bartley came back presently, and helped me to

give our patient sips of milk, which seemed to do him good, though he was not yet conscious. His face became a little less pale, and his heart-beat a little stronger.

"Perhaps we should get the doctor to come," I said doubtfully.

"He couldn't do anything that we can't do," said Bartley. "Keep him warm and get him to drink a drop from time to time. This is not the first time I've seen a man in this condition."

So I heated bricks in the fire and put them against him, and Bartley went back to his own house and brought me some poteen. We rubbed this on his chest as well as making him drink it, but still it was evening before I saw the first sign of returning life.

I had got up to light the lamp. Bartley had gone home for his supper, promising to come back later to see how things were. As I leaned over the table fitting on the glass globe my shadow cut the room in half. This and the smoke-blackened rafters, for there was no ceiling, were the first things the stranger saw as he lay on his back in the settle-bed. With my back still turned to him, I heard a low frightened babbling in a strange language. While I blessed him for being alive, I found time to be irritated that we were not going to be able to understand each other.

I carried the lamp over and stood looking down at him. His eyes were open now, and I thought he looked at me very curiously. I said I hoped he was feeling better, thinking that even if he did not understand me he would recognise from my expression that I meant him no harm. I was surprised and pleased when he answered me in careful English: "Yes, I am better. I have been well treated." He looked around the room. "What place is this?"

"This is Farran, in Connemara. Farran village is quite near, down that way." I pointed to the east. "My name is Pat Hernon."

"And I am Manuel Carrera," he said.

He raised himself on his elbow. I put the pillows behind him so that he could sit up more comfortably. He lay back against them watching me hang the lamp on the wall and put the kettle over the fire for my own supper. Though he had spoken civilly enough, I did not like the way his dark brown eyes darted around me. For a man who had been unconscious all day, and probably half the night as well, they were very agile eyes, and their watchfulness made me uneasy. Still, I knew that he was too weak to do me an injury, so I went on with my supper. I had no real reason for these feelings, but somehow I felt like the man in the story who picked up the frozen viper and warmed it until it revived and bit him.

I hoped I was not showing my feelings in my face. I offered him tea, which he drank eagerly. Then he said casually:

"Where did you find me?"

"On the shore," said I.

He thought for a moment, and then he said: "My clothes are not wet."

"Then you must have had a boat," I said blandly.

"The lifeboat," he said, half to himself. "I remember being in the lifeboat."

He gave a long shudder, so that I almost felt sorry for him. Now it may seem that I should have told him that I had the brig and the lifeboat safe, and that he could have them when he would be well enough. But to me it was not as simple as that. I had a strong impression that the ownership of the brig was doubtful, and before I would consent to tell about it I was determined to hear something of its story.

Manuel studied me for a moment. I pretended not to notice, as I went on with my supper, but I thought that he was busy working out the line that his explanation was to take. He fumbled in his pocket and took out a little black cheroot, which I lit for him with a glowing coal from the fire. He blew a big cloud of smoke and looked at me through it. Then he said: "I suppose a boy of your age notices everything that happens. If an old sailing ship went past out there, I'm sure you would see it."

"It's likely I would," said I.

"I thought so. Now I will tell you a story, and then you will understand why I want to find that sailing ship. You and I could sail her together. There is no one on her, and I will need help."

I got up and went to the fire, so that he would not see my face. While I pulled the sods about with the tongs I said:

"We don't often see sailing ships in these parts."

"No," he said. "No. This is a very old ship. Her name is the *San Sebastian*. I will tell you about her, and I am sure you will help me."

He waited again for me to promise that I would help him, but I said nothing. At last he went on:

"Did you ever hear of a country called Chile?"

"That is in South America, I think."

"Yes. It is a long narrow country on the coast of South America. There is a big port there, called Valparaiso, and the *San Sebastian* was built there in the year 1819."

"Perhaps you do not know that Chile belonged to Spain for a long time. Many of the people still have Spanish names, and they look like Spaniards too. Chile is a rich country, and for many years the Spaniards and the Chileans fought each other for possession of it. Though I have a Spanish name myself, I have to admit that when they conquered them, the Spaniards did not treat the Chileans well. They treated them like slaves or animals, so that at last the people revolted. It was when Mateo de Toro was Governor of Chile, in 1810, that the Chileans at last got a chance of seizing power themselves. They sent Mateo away, and they put seven of their own people in charge of the country instead. Spain could do nothing to help, because she was having a war with France at home. But there were still Spanish troops in Chile, of course, and the next year the Chileans attacked a battalion of them while they were on parade, and there was a battle. That was in

28

Santiago. The same year the people formed their own army, and the General-in-Chief was Juan José Carrera, my great-great-grand-uncle."

I had listened to all this with great interest, though I could not see what it had to do with the *San Sebastian*. I could see that Manuel was watching me anxiously, and I guessed that he was trying to get my sympathy and interest by telling me the whole history of the brig. He was succeeding very well in his object, too, for now I begged him eagerly to go on with his story. He smiled at me with pleasure, showing his strong white teeth, and then went on:

"Juan José Carrera was a fine General. When they had finished their own war, the Spaniards sent a huge army with General Paroja in command. He and Carrera fought two battles, and Carrera won both times. But the Spaniards were not going to let Chile go so easily, and they sent reinforcements. Carrera was defeated at last, and the Spaniards were back in power."

"But they only held the country for three years. They did not change their ways, so that when the General returned with a new army, the people supported him as they had done before. Carrera had got help in Buenos Aires, and now he marched against the Spaniards and completely defeated them in the battle of Chacabuco."

"That was in the year 1817. My great-grandfather was at that battle, though he was only a boy."

"Was he the General's nephew?"

"Yes. He told my grandfather about it and my grandfather told me."

"And was that the end of the fighting?"

"No. The Chileans went to war again to help the people of Peru to get their independence, and succeeded too. Some said they should have attended to their own affairs first, and perhaps they were right. I don't know what happened to General Carrera after the battle. Perhaps he was killed. The first National Governor of Chile was an Irishman."

"An Irishman!"

"Yes. General Ambrose O'Higgins. There is a statue of him in Valparaiso. I saw it myself."

I gave a long sigh of delight. Manuel went on:

"Well, after a few years, the country settled down and became prosperous, with a new Constitution and a national government. And my great-great-grandfather, the general's brother, built the *San Sebastian* in 1819, and used her to trade between Chile and Spain. He carried copper and silver and walnuts, and sometimes alabaster and lapis lazuli. He always carried clean cargoes, because he took such a pride in his ship. He died on board the *San Sebastian* and was buried at sea."

"And who owned her then?"

"His son, my great-grandfather. He never sailed her at all. He brought her into port in Santander, in the north of Spain. He was afraid she was too old even then to sail the Atlantic. He had her for a kind of show-piece. She was still a show-piece, with

30

people coming specially to see her, until she broke her moorings last week when I was on her alone. I could do nothing with her – she's far too big to handle alone – but I hoped that I could steer her away from danger by staying on board. If I saw another ship I meant to hail it and ask for help. Then the storm came up last night, as you saw, and I got frightened. I thought that if she foundered while I was on board, I would be drowned. I'm no sailor, but I've always heard people say that sailors take to the boats in a storm."

He grinned at me again, so frankly that I found myself beginning to trust him, and reproaching myself for my suspicions.

"How did you launch the lifeboat?" I asked.

"There were ropes and things," he said vaguely. "I got it into the water somehow, and climbed down by a rope ladder. I held on to the ladder for a long time, letting the brig pull me along, but I had to let go at last. The brig moved faster than I did. I tried to follow her for a while, but when the storm got worse I lost the oars, and I was thrown about so much that I must have become unconscious at last. I hope she is not broken up already. Perhaps you found pieces of her on the shore?"

I might have told him then if he had not looked at me so craftily. At that moment, Bartley and Mrs Folan lifted the latch and walked in.

"Glory be to goodness!" said Mrs Folan the moment she was inside the door. "Is this the poor man that was washed up by the tide? Tell me now, sir, are you feeling all right? Did they do anything for you at all? It's only this minute Bartley me about you, and I made him come over with me at once to see were you alive or dead. Imagine not telling me all the evening! I could have baked a cake – I could have brought you a raw egg – there's nothing like a raw egg for a man that's washed up by the tide – "

While she fussed over Manuel, Bartley gave me a warning look, as if he knew what I had been about to do. Manuel was smiling and flashing his teeth at Mrs Folan and he did not see me shake my head slightly to show that I had not given away any information. I said:

"He's much better now, ma'am. He was telling me about Chile – "

Now it was Manuel's turn to send me a warning look. It seemed he did not want Bartley to hear the story of the brig. Bartley saw the look, but he pretended to have noticed nothing. He said:

"Have you been to Chile? You're a long way from there now."

"It's a long time since I was there," said Manuel uncomfortably. "The last country I was in was Spain."

"Manuel says that the first governor of the Chilean Republic was an Irishman called O'Higgins," I said eagerly. "He says he saw his statue in Valparaiso."

I am sure it was obvious from my tone that I envied Manuel his travels, for I saw Bartley cock an eye at me.

"I have heard there is a statue of an Englishman there too," he said, "but I've forgotten his name. He commanded the navy about the time of the Revolution. Did you see that statue too?"

"His name is Jones," said Manuel. "It's a well-known statue. Have you been to Chile, señor?"

"My brother that's in America spent a while there," said Bartley. "He used to write and tell us about it. He said the cold at Christmastime would freeze the nose off a brass monkey."

Manuel laughed.

"That's right. I'll never forget Christmas in Chile. I used to long for our warm climate at home in Spain."

"What ship did you come on? Are you a sailorman by trade?"

"No," said Manuel. "I was a passenger. I don't remember much about it except that I was in a lifeboat."

"Well, you're safe as a house now," said Bartley. "Pat will look after you until you're fit to go into Galway and look for a boat home."

Manuel's eyes narrowed with dislike before he managed to grin again.

"Thank you. I will tell my people at home how well I have been received."

Now we could see that Manuel was exhausted, for he was still very weak. Bartley and Mrs Folan went away and I sat on by the fire, saying nothing. Presently I noticed that Manuel had fallen into a doze. I got up very silently and slipped outside to the gable of the house. There, as I had expected, Bartley was waiting for me.

"I thought you'd never come," he said, gripping my arm. "I hope you didn't tell him anything."

"No. I didn't trust him."

"You were right. That man is a liar. He was never in Chile in his life."

"How do you know?"

"He gave away the game on himself. He thought we would know nothing, I suppose. Did you hear him saying there is a statue of an Englishman called Jones in Valparaiso?" I nodded. "Well, it's a statue of Lord Cochrane," said Bartley. My brother told me in a letter."

"But perhaps Manuel forgot," I said doubtfully. "Perhaps he saw the statue but didn't know the man's name. That could happen. He knows a lot about the history of Chile."

"So do I," Bartley pointed out, "and I was never there in my life. I say he never saw that statue at all. Anyway he said another thing that couldn't be just a mistake. Did you hear him agreeing that it's very cold at Christmas in Chile? Well, my bother says that Christmas comes in the middle of summer in Chile! He said it was the queerest thing to see the sun splitting the stones on Christmas morning – what do you think of that?" he asked triumphantly.

I agreed that it proved Manuel a liar. Bartley could not see why he should tell such yarns, until I told him about the history of the *San Sebastian*. Then he said:

"It seems to me that Manuel is very anxious to

make you believe he owns the brig, so that you will help him to save it if it comes in. Now I wonder why that brig is so valuable?"

"He said it was a show-piece. It could be worth a lot of money for that."

"It could so. It's a fine ship. Anyone would want to own it."

Still he sounded doubtful. I told him the rest of Manuel's tale, and I said that I thought Manuel had wanted me to keep it secret. Bartley said:

"It seems to me that Manuel is not a very clever rogue. Wouldn't you think he'd have the sense to know that you would not keep that story to yourself? And look how I saw through him so easily!"

"What will I do with him?" I asked, relieved at this judgement.

"You'll have to let him stay until he's well, anyway. Don't let him see you know anything about the brig, and maybe he'll let fall some information about her himself."

"Perhaps we should let him see her," I said. "I don't like this."

"Is it hand her over to the first thief that comes along with his hand out? On my soul, we won't! If she honestly belongs to him, that will be another story. Now, be sure you don't even look as though you have something on your mind!"

I resolved to take this advice, at any rate, and I watched Bartley stump off before I went into the house again.

3

The Face at the Window

Manuel was still asleep when I went in. I had time to sit in the same place again before he stirred and opened his eyes. He smiled at me in such a friendly way that in spite of Bartley's advice I found it hard to believe him a scoundrel. Then I noticed a triumphant look flit across his face, and my doubts returned again.

"Your neighbours gone?" he asked softly.

"Yes. It is very late."

"Good. You did not tell them about my brig?"

I shook my head.

"Good," he said again. "I do not want everyone to know. It is better not to have everyone knowing a thing like that." He studied me for a moment. "And you will help me?" While I hesitated to answer so direct a question, he fumbled under his clothes and then said: "Come over here, boy. Come over close."

I got up and went over to him where he still lay back against the pillows. He was a little flushed now, and his brown eyes shone with a feverish light. He stretched out his hand towards me, and then opened it suddenly with the palm upwards. I started back in disgust.

Lying in his hand, glowing dully in the soft light of the oil-lamp, were several gold pieces. They were bigger than pennies, and quite thick. While I watched he pushed his hand towards me and said:

"Take them, boy. They are very valuable."

Now I should explain that, though nearly all the Connemara people are miserably poor, they can be as easily and as deeply insulted by the offer of money as many a wealthy man. If you buy a drink for a Connemara man, he is more than likely to buy another for you, and dare you with his eye to refuse it. I had been brought up in this proud tradition by my father and by Bartley, and if Manuel had offered me a sackful of gold, I think I would have been just as scornful. This may seem strange since I was so anxious to own the brig. But that I regarded as an earned right, while Manuel's gold was a bribe. It was a very fine distinction.

Now I noted another thing. Manuel had not seen me start back, nor had he noticed my expression. The reason was that he was looking lovingly at the money in his hand as if he were promising it that it would not be parted from him for long. This thought came into my mind all at once, as I watched his lips pulled back from his teeth in a greedy smile. Bartley had said that Manuel seemed to think that we were ignorant people who could easily be fooled. Now it occurred to me that he might also be stupid enough to think that one of us would never be missed. If I did help him to get possession of the brig, I was sure he would think nothing of sailing me out a piece and then quietly putting me overboard.

The time had come for me to make some answer to the offer. I said:

"I don't need to be paid to help you."

I thought I would have to protest some more, but he closed his hand over the gold pieces at once with a little contemptuous smile which he could not suppress. I turned away, and saw out of the corner of my eye how he fumbled quickly at his waist again as he put the money away. I wondered if he had a money belt under his clothes. I had seen one of these once, that Joe Fahy's uncle had had in Western America.

It was midnight now, and I was very tired. It had been a long and exciting day. I yawned in spite of myself. Manuel said:

"Where are you going to sleep?"

I pointed to the door of the bedroom off the kitchen and told him that I always slept in there.

"You will be warm here by the fire," I said. "I will make it up so that it will stay in all night."

He watched without speaking while I built a wall of turf sods and put the fire in the middle, and then surrounded it with more sods. The he said in a small wavering voice:

"Will you lock the door?"

I looked at him in astonishment. His lips were trembling, and little drops of sweat had appeared on his forehead. From a gay, confident rogue, he had become a shivering, frightened child. Then I remembered that he was still a sick man. I said gently:

"I never lock the door at night. All the people in this neighbourhood are my friends."

"They are not my friends," he said sharply.

"As long as you are in my house they are," I said. "If they wanted to visit me in the middle of the night, I wouldn't like them to find the door locked against them."

I said this as a joke, for of course none of my neighbours would think of disturbing us in the middle of the night. But Manuel cried out:

"No, no! No one must come in! You must lock the doors – all the doors!"

"There are only two," I said quietly. "I'll lock them if you like."

"Yes, yes. Good boy," he said eagerly. "And the windows – what about the windows?"

I said I would latch the window too.

"Is there a window in your bedroom?" he asked. "You must not forget that one."

"But I must have some air," I said, exasperated.

He almost began to cry, as he babbled:

"You can leave the door open. You will get plenty of air through the door. It will come down this

39

chimney." Suddenly he stopped and then whispered: "Down the chimney!" His voice was charged with horror. "It is a very big chimney. Anyone could come in that way."

"It's too small at the top," I said, and he looked relieved.

"Yes, yes. It is too small."

His eyes darted about, looking for other ways by which his unnamed enemies could enter, and at last he seemed satisfied. It would have been cruel to have pointed out that if anyone was determined to come in, he would only have to climb on the roof, make a hole in the soft thatch and drop down on to the floor of the kitchen inside. I was glad that this thought did not occur to Manuel, or I should have had to spend all night by the settle-bed, holding his hand.

He watched me carefully while I secured the doors and windows. No one likes the thought of unknown enemies prowling about a dark house, and by the time I had finished I almost had the jitters myself. I actually got down on my knees and looked under my bed, and I remember the huge relief I felt when no face leered back at me. Then I was ashamed of my foolishness, and it was only later that I began to wonder what I would have done if I had found an unwanted visitor lying in wait for me.

Presently, however, I fell sound asleep, and I did not stir until the morning sun shone in through the window on to my face.

While I was getting into my clothes I could hear

Manuel moving about in the kitchen. When I came out of my room he was standing in the open doorway in the sun. He turned around to wish me good morning, and I saw at once that his courage had returned with the day. He was staring eagerly at the sea, but of course there was no sign of the *San Sebastian*. While we sat at breakfast, he kept getting up and going to the window to look out, but by the time we had finished he seemed to have wearied of this, and he sat staring into the fire while I cleared the cups away.

I was glad to see that he had recovered his strength in some measure, for I hoped that I would soon be rid of his company. I intended to give Bartley the task of asking him to go. Suddenly he looked up at me and shot out a question.

"Do you ever have Norwegian whalers hereabouts?"

"Not here," I said. "They keep more to the Mayo coast. They land the whales on the islands. I have often heard that they go to Inishkee."

"Inishkee? That is an island?"

"Yes."

"Have you ever been there?"

"No, but Bartley has. It's quite a small island."

"Does Bartley know any of the whalers?"

"No. I don't know much about them, but I think the people are a bit afraid of them. Anyway they never have anything to do with them. Not like the trawlermen."

"Ah, the people are friendly with the trawlermen?"

"More than with the whalers anyway."

He paused and meditated. it was clear that he had some connection with the whalers, but whether these were the enemies he had feared last night I could not be sure. At last he said:

"If you see any whalers about here, you'll tell me, won't you?"

"But how will I know them?"

"If you see any strangers tell me, and I will know whether they are whalers or not."

"Do you want them to see you?" I asked suddenly.

"No, no! They must not see me – they must not know I am here at all!"

So it was the Norwegians he feared, I said to myself, and I wondered where they were supposed to fit into the story about the brig being a family heirloom. I said that if I saw any strangers about I would tell him. He thanked me coolly, and again I was amazed at the change in his mood.

He watched me getting ready for the day's work. It was a soft mild day, and since the spring planting was well over, Bartley and I had decided to spend the day on the bog. We each owned a strip of bog on the shoulder of the mountain, and when we had time we cut enough turf for our own needs, and some over for sale as well. It was still too early in the year for turf cutting, but we had planned to bring home part of the huge rick we had built at the bog, and to sell a few loads in Galway on market days.

"What are you going to do?" Manuel asked, as he saw me throw a coil of rope over my shoulder. I told him.

"The bog?" he said. "Is it a long way from here?"

I pointed towards the Minaun mountain. "And you will be gone all day?"

He had seen me put bread and a can of buttermilk into a basket to take with me. I said that we would be up and down from the bog during the day, but that I was bringing the food in case we happened to be too far from home when the time would come for a meal. Then I said:

"Would you like to come with us?"

I could see him thinking this over, weighing the chance of finding the brig against the fear of being found by the whalers. At last he said:

"I don't know. It is a long way."

"We'll give you a ride in the cart," I said, partly to tease him, for I guessed he did not want to come.

"Ah, no." He smiled. "The poor old burro, Simon, would get tired."

"Simon doesn't go to the bog," I said. "He's too old. We'll be bringing Bartley's pony."

I stopped suddenly, and turned away so that he would not see my face. I need not have troubled, for he had gone to the door again to look out at the sea. As I watched him outlined in the bright doorway, I tried to pull my scattered brains together and work out what was next to be done. For now I knew that Manuel had not been quite unconscious yesterday.

Else, how had he known that my old donkey was called Simon?

I tried to remember every word that was spoken last evening. I was certain that the donkey had not been mentioned at all after Manuel had woken up. There had been so many other things to talk of. I had been so excited, of course, that I had not observed Manuel closely enough, and he must have foxed me.

Simon, Simon. Suddenly I remembered. Bartley had come in the door, saying something as he came. He had stopped short at sight of Manuel, and I had told him that I had brought him up from the shore on Simon's back. I had mentioned both the brig and the lifeboat. Even before that, Manuel must have been conscious, because I was sure that neither of us had said that Simon was a donkey! Perhaps he had come to himself while he was on Simon's back, with his head hanging downwards so that the blood ran into it and brought him to. Then perhaps he had become unconscious again. I recalled how I had dropped him into the settle bed, and how he had made no sound. I was certain that he had not stirred at all while I was sitting watching him.

So now he knew that we had the brig, it seemed. Well, there was no help for that, except that he must not find her until we had discovered our legal rights in the matter. She was well hidden, but a determined man who knew what he sought might succeed in finding her. I could see now that he had never expected the brig to come floating along, nor that I would help him sail her in to safety. It was probable that he had simply been hoping that I would let fall some information about where I had hidden her. I was sorry now that I had said so positively that we were going to the bog, but we could not change our plans now without arousing his suspicions. I thought it would be better if he continued to feel that he had tricked us.

I had no difficulty in persuading him to come over to Bartley's house with me. We went by the lane instead of by my usual short cut across the fields, for he still looked to weak to climb walls. We found Bartley harnessing the pony in the sun, at the gable of the house. Mrs Folan made Manuel come in and sit by the fire, and she chattered away to him while she hung on the kettle to make some tea. She always welcomed an excuse for making tea, even right after breakfast, and of course a stranger must be offered hospitality. While she fluttered about, I took the opportunity of slipping out for a word with Bartley, saying that he would need help.

He did not need my help, of course. He had the pony harnessed and ready, and was able to give all his attention to my story. I cut it very short, for I feared that at any moment Manuel might come around the corner and catch us conspiring. Bartley said, as I had expected:

"Didn't I tell you he was a thief and a rogue? An honest man wouldn't have let on to be unconscious."

"Perhaps he thought it was the whalers who had him," I said.

"Maybe." Bartley thought for a moment and then went on: "Well, now we must go to the bog as we said we would. Herself will keep an eye on him while we're away, and do it better than we would ourselves, too."

Presently we led the pony around to the kitchen door, and Bartley called out:

"We're off now, and we're leaving you in charge of each other!"

Mrs Folan appeared at the door as we climbed on the cart.

"I'll look after him like he was a clocking hen," she said. "He'll be nice and quiet resting here. I won't let him walk a step."

Manuel came to the door too, and she laid a hand on his arm while her eyes twinkled at us. As plain as speech, her look said that she would watch him like a gaoler until we would come back.

As we clattered and rumbled up the mountain road, we let the pony set his own course while we watched the house above the shore get smaller and smaller. At first there was no movement there, but after a while Mrs Folan came out and went into the hen-house to collect the eggs. A moment later Manuel came out too, and by his hunched shoulder we read his intention to slip away while her back was turned. Not a moment too soon she turned and saw him. She beckoned him over and made him take the eggs out of her apron and carry them into the house. Then she took his arm and made him help her into the next field, for the egg of the red hen that was laying out. We lay back in the cart with laughter as we watched her pretending to be too stiff to climb the stile that we had seen her hop over a hundred times like a young girl. It was like watching a play, or a puppet-show, rather, since the figures were so small.

The next thing we saw was the Spaniard helping her to carry her big spinning-wheel outside. We guessed that she had despaired of watching him unless he was under her eye all the time, for now she brought out a bag of wool and two carders. She sat him on a creepy-stool by the spinning-wheel and set him to card the wool, which she then spun.

"I can imagine her singing her old spinning-songs to him," said Bartley. "Oh, she's a great woman and no mistake."

That was a half-hearted morning's work for us. When we reached the bog we still had a fine view of Bartley's house, and we were forever straightening up as we loaded the cart to see if Manuel had moved. We need not have worried. Mrs Folan was a fast spinner and to keep up with her he had to keep his carders going without a pause. We guessed that he was new to the task, for occasionally she would bend over him as if she were teaching him how it was done.

We had a fine view of the sea, which had an oily shine on it today. Far out on its pale slate-blue there was a tiny black motionless dot. Someone was fishing from a currach.

"I wonder who that is," said Bartley. "I hope he won't come rowing in when he has finished to take a look at the brig. If he's from Farran he won't because I told them all last night about the stranger being washed up."

But the currach did not move.

When we had a cartload of turf ready we started for home again. Halfway down the mountain I was not surprised to hear Bartley say:

"That will be enough for today. We'll take the laddo fishing in the afternoon. That's one good way of keeping an eye on him."

"Why not send him away into Galway instead?"

"I hear Mr Daly is in Dublin today," said Bartley. "He'll be back tonight, and tomorrow you can get up on the pony and ride into Galway and tell him the whole story. I'll give you a letter for him saying you're not gone out of your mind. You'll be back from Galway in the evening and you'll have word from Mr Daly about what we are to do. Then we'll only have to keep Manuel for one night more, before we say goodbye to him."

This seemed a good plan. I said:

"What if the whalers come looking for him?"

"They'll never find him here," said Bartley. "They have no way of knowing he is in Farran at all. No one from these parts will help him, you may go bail, and as for Manuel himself, he will be anxious enough to keep out of sight, from what you tell me. I'd give a good fishing-net to know what they're all up to."

When we turned into Bartley's yard both Mrs Folan and Manuel heaved huge sighs of relief.

"He hasn't walked a step all morning, hardly," she told us proudly. "I told him he'd be better resting. And I gave him the wool to card because an idle mind is the devil's workshop!"

Manuel smiled at us in a rather sick-looking way and remarked that all knowledge is power, and that he had learned a useful trade since last we saw him. We saw that he was wearing one of Bartley's old jerseys, and I guessed that our early summer sun had not been warm enough for him. Still he jumped at Bartley's suggestion that he should come fishing with us in the afternoon.

"You're not afraid to go, after what happened to you?" said Bartley.

"I am afraid," said Manuel simply. "But a man who is in a strange country cannot afford a fear like that."

We all had dinner together in Bartley's kitchen. Mrs Folan boiled eggs for Manuel, because he was a foreigner and a sick man. But for herself and for us she poured a mountain of steaming potatoes on to the table and provided us each with a piece of salt ling and a fork to eat with. We had lovely old plates with fat pink roses on them, and huge mugs to match, full of buttermilk. While we ate, the hens poked their jerky heads in the door and looked at us. They knew that whatever we left would come to them, and I always fancied that they became anxious if our appetites were good.

Afterwards we moved over to the fire, and Bartley had a smoke. That kind of dinner dulls the wits somewhat, and makes one sleepy, and we were in no hurry to move. It amused us to watch Manuel's impatience. He went to the door a hundred times until at last Mrs Folan said:

"I always heard the Spaniards were slow kind of people. Maybe it's the cooler air in Ireland, sir, but you're like a hen on hot bricks, so you are. Sit down there a while and take your ease, or I won't let you go fishing at all!"

That quieted him at once. It was obvious that he had developed a fine respect for her in the course of the morning.

At last Bartley got up slowly and put away his pipe. He got down his lines from their place above the fire and passed them slowly through his fingers. Then he had to inspect the hooks and take a can for bait. At last we were ready to go, and as we went to the door Manuel let out a long breath, like the air going out of a balloon, so that Bartley winked at me with delight.

Some of Manuel's eagerness evaporated when he saw the boat in which we were to put to sea. He said:

"Is that the boat you usually fish from?"

"It is," said Bartley. "A fine boat. I made it myself."

"Is that one out there the same?"

He pointed to the black dot which we could still see, though it had drifted a little to the west since the morning. Bartley nodded, and Manuel looked from the distant currach to the one on the water's edge. Then without a word he stepped over the gunwale and clambered up to the bows, where he sat on the floor looking quietly terrified.

Bartley and I took a pair of oars each, and in a moment we were skimming over the still water. Presently Bartley stopped rowing and let down a line, while I pulled along slowly. We had kept away from the neighbourhood of the cave, of course, lest by chance any part of the brig might be visible. Now we saw that Manuel was looking eagerly along the line of the shore, and presently he began to question Bartley about the houses and villages that he could see shining white against the background of rocky fields.

"There is a quay at Farran village," said Bartley. "We'll go there tomorrow evening, maybe, if you'd like to see it."

Just then a mackerel bit on the line, and Bartley hauled him in. When we turned around again, Manuel had a pair of field-glasses in his hand, and was searching the coast with them. We could see that he knew it would be difficult to hide a brig the size of the San Sebastian for any length of time. I heartily wished that I could have gone to Galway today, for I knew that precious time was being wasted.

We made a poor enough catch that afternoon – a few more mackerel and an unlucky rock-fish that had wandered too far afield. Manuel never once took his eyes off the line of the shore. There was nothing for him to see, but he did not seem to lose interest for all that. The sea remained as calm as a sheet of ice, and one could hardly see the line in the far distance where it met the sky. Towards evening we saw a small trawler on its way into the bay. A thin curl of vapour hung in the air like a question mark, after it was gone. The other currach had long since disappeared when Bartley said:

"Well, I think we'll get no more here."

He hauled in his line and took his pair of oars again, and we pulled for home. Manuel was looking at us in a puzzled way, and I thought he was about to ask a question. But he must have changed his mind, for he said nothing at all on the way in. I guessed that he must be disappointed, and a hard knot between his eyes seemed to show that he was determined not to waste any more time. I could see that Bartley had observed this too. I knew he would be pleased, for I had often heard him say that an angry man is his own worst enemy.

We carried the currach high out of the water's reach and went up to Bartley's house. Mrs Folan made a great fuss over the fish, as if we had made a wonderful catch. She cooked some, and we all had supper together.

It was nine o'clock when Bartley said:

"It's getting dusky. The boys will be dropping in soon, and I'm thinking Manuel won't be feeling like chatting with them. Tomorrow evening, when you're stronger, you can tell them all about yourself and how you came to be here. You may be sure they'll insist on hearing everything."

I guessed that Bartley wanted us to go, lest some of the "boys" let fall a remark that would show that we all knew where the brig was hidden. Manuel was not anxious to be questioned. He got up at once and suggested that we be getting home.

I found myself quite reluctant to leave the cheerful fire and the feeling of security that filled the house. Here the door could stand open to let in the soft evening light. I knew that my doors would be shut fast for the evening and the spirit of fear locked within to keep us company.

Trying to look light-hearted, I followed Manuel, who had already gone outside. Bartley said softly:

"I'll be over later on to see that you're all right."

I hoped he did not notice how grateful I felt for this promise.

Manuel was waiting for me at the top of the boreen. I made him come with me by the short cut, however, and found that he was as well able to climb the walls as myself. My house looked blind and dark and somehow frightening when we reached it. I found myself shivering a little as I opened the door. It would not have surprised me to have found a company of strange, hostile men sitting around my kitchen table. The fire was down, and the grey light from the door and the tiny window did not reach the corners. I stepped into the kitchen. Manuel, breathing like an animal, was hardly a step behind me. I looked about the room and was vastly relieved to find it empty. I bolted the outer door, in an agony while I worked the bolt up and down. It was so rarely used that it was stiff with rust.

Still I did not feel secure. There was a sort of tightness in the air which I could not explain. I was impatient with myself for being such a fool. Then I blamed Manuel, who was crouching with his back to the wall. How could anyone be at ease, I thought, while his eye could rest on such a personification of terror? He was bent at the waist, with his body pressed against the wall and one ear cocked to listen. His hands were outspread, the palms flat on the door. His knees were acrook and his feet lifted on their toes as if they were ready for flight. In the gloom I could see that his dark face had turned a horrid yellow. Suddenly I sprang forward and opened my bedroom door. The room was empty and looked just as I had left it.

"There is no one here but ourselves," I said and wondered why my voice shook.

Manuel straightened up, but he still stood by the wall. I knelt before the fire and raked it out, and then I put on some turf. I did not make a big fire, for I could see that we were going to spend the evening battened under hatches. When I had the fire going I reached up for the wall lamp and brought it to the table. Manuel spoke for the first time, croaking like a scald crow:

"Do not light that lamp!"

I took off the globe and laid it on the table.

"It's bad enough to be locked in," I said. "I'm not going to sit in the dark, like a rat."

"Do not light that lamp, I say!"

The mixture of anger and fear in his voice made me pause for a moment. The I said boldly:

"This is my house. If I want a light I'll have it."

And I struck a match and put it to the wick.

Manuel lunged forward to stop me. In the wind of his movement, the lamp flared up in a tall, smoky flame like a dragon's tongue. The globe rolled to the floor, where it tinkled to pieces. I gave a wild shout:

"Look out! You'll set the house on fire!"

He clapped his bare hand on top of the flame and quenched it. It was in that moment before the light went out that I looked up and saw the face at the window.

4

Erik

I felt myself grow cold and stiff, as though a chill wind had blown through the room. The short hairs on the back of my neck twitched a little. My staring gaze refused to leave the window. It seemed to me that the eyes of the watcher were fixed on mine. For a full minute we stood thus, and then the face moved a little sideways, as if to peer more closely into the room. I realised then that from outside the kitchen must be as dark as a rat-hole.

I could not be sure yet that Manuel had seen the watcher. I wondered if the watcher had seen him in the light of the lamp. My instinct had been sure, after all, and I blamed myself for not having trusted to it. Still, I had bolted the door, and the windows were latched. But these fortifications would be worthless against even one determined man.

How many were there, I wondered? Manuel had seemed to expect several. I thought it likely that this was one of the Norwegian whale-fishers he had mentioned. The moon was up, and I had seen high cheekbones and silvery fair hair sharply outlined in it's light.

Suddenly Manuel's hand grasped my elbow, and I knew he had seen the head that still filled the lower half of the window. He did not speak, for which I was grateful, and his breathing seemed to have stopped. Then all at once, the head vanished silently. Manuel gave a little moan. I shook him off my arm and took stock of my position.

Here I was, caged into my own house, with a stranger about whom I knew nothing. He had some quarrel with the people outside, but which party was in the right was a mystery to me. I was being forced into taking Manuel's side, but for all I knew Manuel might attack me at any moment if the fancy took him. Of one thing only I was certain: that I did not want his gore staining my kitchen floor, and I was determined that there would be no fighting if I could prevent it. I knew, however, that if there were a fight I would be fighting for the brig, and I had so fallen in love with her that I could not even now grudge her the pass in which I found myself. I had risked my life before for smaller prizes – a basking shark, a floating sea-chest in a storm. What were these to the *San Sebastian*?

I wished I had curtains for the windows. Their usefulness had never before occurred to me. Then I thought that I would try the enemy's game myself. I darted away from Manuel, for I guessed that he would try to stop me, and went to the side of the window. Flattened against the wall, I edged forward cautiously until I could see sideways through the glass. A second later I had shrunk back again, my heart in my mouth.

Standing in front of the window, with their heads together in conference, there were three men. The ground fell away behind them, so that they were silhouetted against the sky. A peaceful moon sailed above them and threw a silver path on the sea. In that moment, too, I had seen the riding lights of a small trawler at anchor below the house. This was how they had come, then. It seemed likely that it was the same trawler that we had seen earlier in the day, on its way into the bay. Usually the trawlers never put in except in bad weather, or when they had engine trouble, or a member of the crew sick.

Manuel came over to me and hissed:

"Did you see anyone?"

"Yes. Three."

Again he moaned and prayed in Spanish. I told him to be quiet, that we had not yet come to the end of our resources. I thought he would lick my hand in gratitude.

The fire was beginning to blaze a little now, and I dowsed it with ashes. I went back to the window again and peered out. The men were not to be seen now. I remembered my thought of the night before, and hoped that they had not climbed on the roof. Manuel slithered towards me. As he crossed a beam of moonlight on the floor, the whites of his eyes gleamed.

Just as he reached me, a single tap sounded on the door. It was so soft that I could not be sure I had heard it at all. It was not a knock, but a soft sound of metal on wood. A knife? The idea sent a shiver through me, and then a flare of anger. The tap sounded again, louder this time. Still neither of us moved. As long as they do no more than knock, thought I, we need not worry about them. It seemed likely that they did not want to attract attention by making a loud noise.

For the third time we heard the tap on the door. Then a voice outside called out:

"Manuel Carrera!"

It was a high, light voice, a singer's voice, and it spoke the name caressingly, as if it were part of a song.

There was no uncertainty about it, and no question. Manuel took a step towards the door, but I caught his arm and whispered:

"Don't answer."

"The door is locked," said Manuel, half to himself.

Since this seemed to comfort him, I did not tell him how easily it could be smashed in.

There was a pause while we listened to each other's breathing. Then the voice called out again:

"Manuel! Manuel Carrera!"

When there was no reply from within, the man seemed to come closer to the door so that he need not speak so loud. The he started off on a long singsong speech in Spanish which I did not understand, but which sent Manuel into a fit of the horrors. Once the man outside stopped and laughed like a devil. Then he went on again with what he had to say.

I pulled Manuel across the room to the back wall. He was a good deal stronger than I was, but he came like a led bull. He was shaking all over, and I thought him quite capable of rushing out to his enemies and being slaughtered on my doorstep. It occurred to me that I might come to the same end.

I shoved him into the corner behind the settle. I could not see him in the pitch dark. I whispered urgently:

"What is all this? What did he say? Whisper – don't talk aloud."

"How did he find you?"

"He found an empty bean-tin on the rocks. Did you hear him knock on the door with it?"

I nearly laughed out loud. There was the knife I had imagined. I had never yet heard of anyone being stabbed with an empty bean-tin. My amusement lasted about five seconds, before it occurred to me that a man has two hands. Why should he not have a bean-tin in his left and a knife in his right? Another thought ran into my head. Manuel should know for certain now that someone had explored the brig. He would surely remember that he had last seen that tin on board. What an idle fool I had been not to leave it there! Manuel was going on:

"He says he saw me in the light of the lamp. He says that if I come out they won't harm me, but I must tell them where the brig is. If I don't come out they will get at me some time, sooner or later, he says – "

Again he took to shivering and stammering. I did my best to soothe him down, for I thought he would be more manageable if he were less frightened. Suddenly he said:

"And I don't know where the brig is. They'll never believe that. *You* know where it is! Tell me at once, or I'll slit you open!"

I cut short his threats by saying as coolly as I could:

"One enemy should be enough for you to handle. If your friends outside will go away, we may start a quarrel of our own in peace."

This was a brave-sounding statement, but in fact I was bogged down in difficulties now. On the whole I thought that if I had to fight at all, I would prefer a fight with Carrera, but only because there were three of the others. I was no nearer to knowing who owned the *San Sebastian*. I could guess that Manuel had stolen it from the people outside, but they did not look like respectable ship-owners. And if they were sure of their legal rights, why had they not called the police or they navy or whoever deals with such things? Then they could have had the satisfaction of seeing Manuel hauled off in chains to gaol. I said:

"Do you know the man outside?"

"The one that spoke? Yes, I know him."

"Who is he?"

"A Norwegian. Erik Vifilson."

"What language did he speak?"

"He spoke Spanish. He knows Spanish well. They all do."

"Is he a whale-fisher?"

"Yes, yes."

Suddenly Manuel was clinging to me again and imploring me to save him. It was as if answering my questions about Erik had heightened his fear of him again. It was obvious that he realised that he had less to fear from me and my friends. I patted him and whispered to him and told him not to speak, and he said he would not.

Just then Erik piped up again:

"Manuel!" There was a pause before he went on, to my surprise, in careful English: "Manuel, do you hear me? Pat Hernon, do you hear me?"

I jumped in my skin, and it seemed as if a cold, wet toad had landed on the back of my neck. We stood as still as death, side by side, without speaking.

"Pat Hernon, send Manuel outside and you will go free. Send Manuel Carrera outside. He is a thief."

A hopeful pause followed. I wondered if they really expected me to open the door and thrust Manuel outside like a puppy-dog. I could not have done so, even if I had wished. The voice went on:

"We have no quarrel with you, Pat Hernon. Do not shelter Manuel."

62

I wondered why Manuel did not call out to them that I knew where the brig was. If they were all banded together against me, my chances would be worth nothing. I waited momently for him to do this, and I almost gave myself up for lost. But Manuel said nothing still. Either he was greedy to have the brig all for himself, or else Erik had done the business of threatening him far too well, so that he was too terrified to trust him at all.

All at once, we heard the door shiver as a shoulder struck it. I braced myself for the attack, for I knew that door would not stand much of this treatment. Then we heard low, excited voices in an argument. The assault was not repeated. We edged over to the door. Manuel said, after a moment, that he did not understand what they were saying, as they spoke Norwegian. Someone ran around to the back and tried the door there, half-heartedly. I could not make out why they delayed, why they did not break down that door and pick out the pair of us like periwinkles out of the shell.

Then Manuel said:

"They are going away!"

We rushed to the window. It was true. We could see them in the moonlight. They were going down towards the shore. As we crowded each other in the window for a view, they moved swiftly down the hill, never once looking back. Manuel said, in a kind of shivering scream:

"They do not need to look back. They see everything. They know everything!"

"Stop that!" I said. "Do you want them to hear you?"

He stopped chattering, but he could not take his eyes off the three men. Soon their heads dropped below the brow of this hill, and they were out of sight. We waited perhaps three minutes, and then a boat drew out from the shore. It crossed the track of the moon and made for the trawler. Presently it slid up against the trawler and became part of the darkness. It was too far away for us to see, but I could imagine the men climbing aboard like eels. Still we waited. I wished Manuel would not blow down my neck. Then in the still air we heard the faint sound of an anchor-chain. The trawler swung around, trailing the row-boat, and started back eastward, the way she had come. She made good speed, and in a few minutes she had gone out of sight behind the reef.

"They are gone," said Manuel joyfully. "They're all gone." He laughed shakily and then said, with an attempt at recovering my respect: "They are very dangerous fellows. It would not be sensible not to fear them."

I agreed dryly, and then remarked:

"They do not mean to go far."

"How do you know?"

"They are trailing their dinghy. If they meant to go a long way they would surely take it on board."

"That is true. Then they may be coming back."

"Very likely."

"You told everyone I was here – you and your stupid old neighbour. Perhaps you sent word to the whalers."

"Nonsense! How could I have known they would be interested?"

"You are in league with them. You are all in league with them!"

He was becoming hysterical again. I was at my wits' end what to do with him. I thought he must be the sorriest, most unbusiness-like rogue in the world.

"It looks as if you will have to choose between me and them," I said. "If you injure me, my friends will see to it that no one from these parts will help you. Then you will very soon fall into the hands of the whalers."

"Tell me where my brig is hidden!" he said threateningly.

"What use would that be?"

"Ah! So you know where she is! I would sail her away, of course!"

"All alone? In a flat calm? Has she an engine?"

He was taken aback at this thought, which had not occurred to him. I could almost hear his brain churning beside me in the darkness. At last he said craftily:

"Take me to the brig and then we will make plans. You could help me to sail her. You saw that I have money to reward you."

"I like to make plans first and act later," I said.

"What is your plan?"

This time his tone was coaxing. I wished we could light the lamp, so that I could watch his face. The thought flitted into my mind that while we talked he could be fingering a knife all unknown to me, in readiness for the moment when he would decide that I was no more use to him. I said:

"You must know by now that I want to help you. I can send a message to the police in Galway. They will send someone at once to protect you better than I can."

"No, no!"

There was no mistaking his opinion of this idea.

"Why not?" I asked innocently. "That is what the police are for. You can explain to them that the brig is yours and that the whalers want to steal it from you. They will be just as ready to help you as if you were an Irishman."

Of course I knew that he would not agree to this. But if by chance he had, my rights would have been safeguarded too. He hardly knew what to answer me. At last, after he had stammered for a bit, he said:

"The police are very good, very worthy people. Everyone knows that the Irish police are very fine people. But they would not understand about my brig."

I smiled sourly to myself. Now I was certain that Manuel had something to fear from the law. I had no way of finding out what this was, but I felt that if I could put off his finding of the brig for a few days, I would be more sure of my ground. I still had no intention of leading him to the brig and handing it over to him.

"I have another idea," I said, "if you do not want to go to the police. I can put you into a hiding-place that your enemies will never think of."

"A grave, perhaps?"

"No!" I shouted. "How can you expect me to help you when you talk like that?"

"I am sorry. What place is it? See how they found me here, and even knew your name."

I had no hiding-place in mind. If fact I had only one idea, and that was to get Manuel out of my house and away with all speed. I could have hidden him in any one of a dozen caves in the mountains or on the sea-shore, but of course I could not guarantee that he would not be found.

"There are sheep-caves," I said. "They would not think of looking for you there."

"They would think of anything," said Manuel simply.

"Suggest something yourself, then," I said pettishly.

"There are sheep-caves in Spain and in Norway too," he said placatingly. "I think it would be better for me to stay here."

"But they will come back and break their way in."

"We will fight them, you and I and the good Bartley."

"Bartley is too old to fight. And why should he? A moment ago you were calling him my 'Stupid old neighbour!'"

But this reminded me that Bartley had said he would come later in the evening. Though it had felt like an age, I knew it was not long since we had left Bartley's house. Still, if he got uneasy about me, he might come along at any moment. I did not want him to stand siege with us in the house. Neither did I want him to walk into the arms of our attackers, who, I felt sure, would not scruple to carry him off as a hostage. Now I knew what I wanted to do, and I was determined to have my way.

"I am going over to Bartley's house for help," I said, and I went towards the door.

I had been right about the knife. He was after me in a flash, and he had the steel at my neck.

"Don't touch that door!"

It is very hard to argue reasonably with six inches of pointed steel at your throat. I gurgled like a baby for half a minute before I was able to speak. Then I said:

"How can I get help if I don't open the door?"

He took the knife away, though he still held my arm. He said:

"How do I know I will ever see you again?"

"You don't know," said I, "but you'll have to risk it."

"You are only a boy," he said, half to himself.

I could not be sure what he meant by this, whether he thought that he could hold me against my will, or that he felt that I was too young to be well versed in villainy. Either way, I was weary of being held prisoner by him. I tried again to impress him with the urgency of getting help.

"They may come back at any moment," I said. "Perhaps they will bring others with them. If I go now, I can be back in a few minutes with a small army of men from the village. They won't have a chance against us all."

"You think the people of the village will help?"

"Of course they will, if Bartley and I ask them."

Again he had to think this out, while the precious moments passed. At last he said, as he let go of my arm:

"Very well, then. Go quickly."

I did not need this advice. I sprang to the door and worked at the bolt. Behind me, Manuel twittered like an old woman, while he urged me on. At last I got it open and swung the door back. The night air that came in against me was the sweetest I ever breathed.

I slipped outside quietly, and then paused to hear Manuel whisper after me:

"Come back as quickly as you can!"

The next moment the door was shut again, and I heard the bolt shudder back into place.

5

Manuel Departs

I flashed over the stile into the field like a stone from a catapult. I was barefoot, as I always was in summertime, and I remember clutching the cool, sweet grass between my toes in a kind of ecstasy of freedom. Then I turned a somersault on the grass and lay there afterwards, staring out to sea.

There was still no trawler in sight. I wondered where it had gone. It occurred to me that I should have told Manuel to watch while I was away, and to come out into the open if he saw the whalers returning. Nothing would have induced me to go back and warn him now. In any case I doubted if he would have taken my advice. It seemed to me that he would be too frightened to save himself. I wondered what he was doing in my absence. The thought crossed my mind that if he were not afraid to use a light he would be searching through my few papers. Then I felt ashamed of myself because I was even now dallying when I should have been on my way to get help for him.

I got up and went on across the field, but a little more slowly than when I had started out. It had suddenly occurred to me that the whalers might have left a sentry. In the dimness of the moonlight, every dark patch of shadow became a crouching man. Every rock hid an assassin. It was agony to climb the next stile and stand poised in full view, even for a second, on top. When I jumped to the ground into the next field my hands were clammy with sweat. I looked wildly to right and left, and then I bolted across that field like a midge-tormented colt. I flung myself over the last stile and into Bartley's yard with my breath coming in short gasps. I shot into Bartley's kitchen and flung the door shut. Then with my back against the door, I looked across the room.

There was no one there but Mrs Folan. She had stood up at my wild entrance, the sock she was knitting trailing from her hand. The light turf ashes that the slammed door had disturbed whirled about her feet. All at once I felt ashamed of having frightened her, and I began to apologise for it.

"Never mind that," she said quickly. "What has happened?"

I told her as best I could and said that I had come to get help from Bartley.

"Is it to go and fight the whalers with you?"

"That is what Manuel wants," I said, "but what I want is to get Manuel away into hiding so that they won't get him."

71

"Why not let them get him?" said Mrs Folan calmly. "Then they could have their quarrel out between themselves."

"But Manuel is so silly," I said. "I don't want him to be caught."

"That is not a good reason," said she. "Still, I suppose we must do something for him."

"Where is Bartley?"

"Gone to Farran for some rope and a gallon of oil. And you're not going after him," she added, as I started towards the door. "What would you do if you met the whalers on the way? You sit down by the fire and wait until Bartley comes back. I'll make some tea."

"But Manuel — "

"Never mind about Manuel. By the look of him I'd say this is not the first time he has found himself in a tight corner."

This was probably true, but I did not think it let me off the obligation to help him. I had promised to come back with help within a few minutes. I had been so sure of finding Bartley and a crowd of his friends here, all ready to run back to my house with me. Short of engaging in a hand-to-hand battle with Mrs Folan, I was imprisoned here now until Bartley's return. I went across and sat on the hob by the fire.

"That's right," said Mrs. Folan comfortably. "We'll have a quiet cup of tea before Bartley comes."

"Where are the boys?" I asked. "I thought I'd find a few of them here."

"They will probably come with Bartley," she said.

"I suppose they started up some old gossip below in Matt Faherty's shop, and they couldn't tear themselves away."

By the scathing tone of her voice one would think she never listened to the latest news herself. I guessed she had been impatiently awaiting the arrival of the company when I had come in. I knew she would be pleased to have news more startling to them than they would hear in Matt's shop in a twelvemonth. I huddled more closely into the chimney-corner, glad in spite of myself of the delay. Of course, it would have been nonsense for me to go back to my house alone.

Still, it was dreadful to have to wait while the kettle came to the boil, and I thought the tea would choke me. Mrs Folan drank hers with all the outward signs of her usual enjoyment, but an anxious light in her eye told me that she was uneasily counting the flying minutes. Though it seemed much longer, only a quarter of an hour had passed before we heard voices outside. Then Bartley was in the kitchen, with half-a-dozen men crowding behind him. He came over to me at once.

"What is wrong? Why is the kitchen door shut?"

Again I repeated my story, to the accompaniment of wondering and sardonic comments from the men.

"And this Norwegian knew your name," said Bartley. "That's a very strange thing."

"But he said he didn't mean me any harm if I gave over the Spaniard to him," I pointed out. "I don't know why they did not shove in the door there and then and take him away with them."

"Maybe they didn't want to make noise," said Ned Donnelly, the blacksmith.

"I think that was it," I said.

"No, no!" said Mrs Folan, and all the men turned to listen to her with respect. "If it was the noise, why didn't they fear to call out to Pat and the Spaniard in the house? You may be sure those laddoes wouldn't be afraid of making noise. I'd say the only thing that would frighten them would be one of their own people, more wicked than themselves!"

"You're right. Mrs Bartley is right," said all the men, nodding to each other.

"So I think they went away in the trawler to tell their leader they had found Manuel," she continued. "They didn't rightly know what to do next – whether to kill him, or capture him, or what – and they knew they would only have to ask the leader and he'd tell them."

"If that's true, the boss can't be far off," said Bartley. "They wouldn't go all the way back to Spain to ask a question like that, leaving Manuel in the house behind them."

"Did anyone see another boat today?" asked Bartley.

No one had, though several of them had seen the trawler. Then Joe Fahy bustled his way to the front of the group and said importantly:

"I know where the trawler spent the evening."

He looked with delight at all the interested faces before he went on:

"My nephew, Tomsy, was over fishing east of the reef in his currach, and he saw the trawler lying all quiet-like in Henry's Cove."

Henry's Cove was a tiny inward curve of the coast on the Galway side of the reef. It was said that an English pirate called Henry had been wrecked there, perhaps two hundred years ago. To hear the people talk about it you would think it had happened yesterday.

"He saw the trawler!" said Bartley. He turned to me. "Then that must have been Tomsy's currach we saw from the bog, and later on when we were fishing ourselves."

"That's right," said Joe. "Tomsy saw you, too. He fished outside for a bit, and then he came in and landed on the reef. If there was anyone on board the trawler, they didn't stir all the time Tomsy was watching."

I wondered if the whalers were simple enough to think that the trawler would not have been noticed. Or perhaps they were so sure of themselves that they did not care who saw them.

Bartley was questioning Joe Fahy again.

"Did Tomsy see anyone going out to the trawler?"

"No," said Joe in a disappointed tone. "I told him he should have watched longer, but he said" – Joe's voice was heavy with contempt – "he said he was hungry for his tea!"

"Never mind, Joe. He saw plenty. Now men!" Bartley began to marshal them as if for battle. "Every man take a weapon!"

They crowded over to the pegs where the farm implements hung, and each took one. A formidable army they looked then with hay-forks, shovels, four-pronged graipes and sleáns at the ready. Mrs Folan was horrified.

"Surely you won't be going to hit the people with those things!" she cried.

"We will if we get half a chance," said Ned Donnelly.

"If we don't hit them they'll hit us," said Joe Fahy fiercely.

He was staggering under a pitchfork taller than himself.

Since he was a man with a trade, he had no skill in handling a farm tool. The others held theirs lightly, and they all looked ready to toss a Norwegian or a Spaniard on them as easily as they would a sop of hay.

"Pat is not to go with you," said Mrs Folan suddenly.

Before an argument could start up, I darted across the kitchen and out the door. The men all streamed out after me, and as I waited for them at the stile I could hear Bartley's voice inside soothing his wife and telling her we would be back in a few minutes to tell her how the battle went. The he told her to sit down quietly there by the fire and go on with her

76

knitting. By the sound of her voice I thought it very unlikely that she would take that advice.

Bartley was first over the stile, and we marched in formation across the field, six men and myself. No one spoke. As we went, my former terror came back to me, and I seemed to live again the horrors of the evening. It was good to be surrounded by such stalwart friends. Without them, I doubt if I would have consented to visit my house again until daylight.

At the second stile, we paused to look out to sea. The moon had clouded over now, and though a sort of glow gave us enough light, the sea was quite dark. The flickering shadows here and there only made it more obscure and confusing.

"There could be a navy of trawlers out there," said Bartley in a low voice, after a moment, "and we wouldn't see them."

We listened for the sound of an engine, but we could hear nothing except the low wash of the waves on the shore. I thought of the *San Sebastian*, the cause of all our trouble, lifting up and down on those same waves in her cave, like some solemn-faced, dreamy lady in an old-fashioned dance. With all my heart I longed to visit her, and I promised myself that come what might, tomorrow would not pass without my seeing her again. As if he could read my thoughts, Bartley said into my ear:

"You need not worry about the brig, Pat. I went around to her this evening before I went into Farran. She's as snug as a bug in a rug, so she is."

I did not like such a homely simile to be used about her, but it brought me down to earth again.

We crossed the second field without a word. The men tried to move noiselessly in their heavy boots. At the second stile we paused again, and still no one spoke. The whitewash of the house gleamed dully ten yards away from us. Between there was grass, and a black turf-stack against the gable. The stile was opposite the gable, so that we could see neither the front nor the back doors. There was no a sound to be heard. Even my hens were fast asleep in their little shed behind the house.

Bartley got over the stile first and crept towards the back of the house. I followed, and then all the others in single file. Someone's sleán rang on stone, and its owner silenced it with his hand.

Everyone paused for a moment. I pictured Manuel crouched inside the house, hearing the sound and not knowing whether the people outside were friends or foes. Bartley moved on again, and we all followed him around to the back of the house. There was a door here, but no windows. I pressed my ear to the door, but I could hear nothing. We went on, and came around to the other gable.

Now a new hazard presented itself. Against this gable I had a small lean-to-shed full of ducks. Usually I collected them from their splashing place on the shore at sundown, drove them up before me and locked them into their shed for the night. This evening, however, I had forgotten all about them, and they must have rambled home in their own good time and waddled into their shed. But they had not been able to shut the door on themselves. Ducks are the silliest little brutes in the world. Now they came tumbling out around our feet, quacking and cheering and hoping it was breakfast-time. They went frantic with rage when they found a dozen boots shoving them aside, stepping on their big flat feet and knocking the feathers out of their little turned-up tails. They shrieked abuse and threats, like a crowd of tinker-women on market-day.

"That's finished it!" shouted Bartley. "To the front door, quick!"

We flung ourselves around the corner. Out from the house leaped three figures, staggering under the weight of a fourth. Even burdened as they were, the were too quick for us. Instead of making for the sea, they shot around the corner of the house.

"After them!" roared Joe Fahy.

When we reached the gable they were already in the lane. We heard a horse's hooves plunging about and the iron-rimmed wheels of a trap grinding on sand. A gun flashed from the back of the trap, as it began to move away. At that moment the moon sailed out from behind the clouds. The horse danced on its hind legs with fright. I saw its wild mane tossing in the moonlight. Its front hooves pawed the air for a moment, and then it bolted away into the darkness with the trap bumping and swaying after it on the stones.

Bartley pulled back Ned who was apparently prepared to run after the trap.

"Let them be," he said. "If they want Manuel that bad, they may as well have him. It's not as if we wanted him ourselves."

"It's a pity we were late," said Johnny O'Neill.

"Maybe 'twas a good thing," said the tailor. "I could never like being shot at."

So they half-joked among themselves as we walked back to the house. I was thinking of Manuel, who might have been safe now if I had not allowed myself to be delayed. I did not even know whether he was alive or dead, and though I had had no cause to love him, my heart ached for his present fate.

All the men agreed that Manuel was a good riddance.

"Of course they may come back," said Joe Fahy.

"I say they won't," said the tailor. "If they meant to come back they wouldn't have fired the shot. That's a reckless class of a thing to do."

"Maybe so. But it could have been an accident."

At the front of the house we all paused. The door was open, and Bartley went in first and struck a light. The lamp still stood on the kitchen table, where I had left it. He put the match to the wick, and a wavering flame flickered around the room.

"The globe is broken," I said, and stopped.

The room was a wreck. To begin with, the door hung sideways off its hinges, having been smashed in as I had predicted. The chairs were flung about and had been left lying on their sides. One leaned lazily against the wall, its front legs off the ground. On the floor at the foot of the dresser there was a heap of broken delph. I could have wept over the lustre jugs that had been my mother's pride. Even the two leering china dogs on the mantel had been knocked over. One lay on his side up there, looking mournfully down at his shattered companion on the hearth.

"Well, if this doesn't beat all," said Joe Fahy softly at last.

"It's like the wreck of the *Hesperus*," said the tailor, who was something of a literary man.

"It looks as if there was a fight," said Ned. "I wonder is the Spaniard gone to Glory."

"There's no blood," said Lazy Johnny cautiously. "And I'd say that if they killed him they wouldn't bother to take him away with them."

"They might," said Bartley. "They might not want the Guards to find his remainders here." He turned to me, "Did you think Manuel was capable of fighting for his life? From what you said, I thought he was so frightened that he would have given himself up to anyone."

"That was what I thought myself," I said.

I was puzzled at this side of the business. The shivering Manuel that I had left behind would not have had the heart to fight three men, up and down a dark kitchen. Suddenly I said:

"I wonder if they were searching for something."

"Ah," said Bartley. He looked around him. "Yes, that would be more likely. Searching for something and not finding it, and then smashing up everything in a temper."

"That's right," said the tailor. "I was wondering how the china dogs got into the fight. Sure, they would be looking down on the heads of the people. Someone put up his hand and knocked them over, I'll be bound."

"Ay, and the jugs and cups off the dresser. Oh, they're a bad lot! Anyone that would take down the lovely jugs and smash them – "

They looked at the pieces and then pityingly at me. Bartley said quickly:

"Pat is well off to have his life. He can spare the delph."

"I wonder where did they go?" said Roddy Moloney, a big quiet man from the other side of Farran. "And where did they get the horse?"

"'Twas a huge horse," said Joe Fahy eagerly. "There's no horse that size in these parts. Did you hear the clamper he made, and the awful height of him when he reared up? Man, he was a terrible big brute altogether!"

The men grinned to each other. It was a secret joke among them that Joe was always impressed with big things, because he was so small himself.

"I have another idea," said Ned Donnelly. "Maybe Manuel was only letting on to be afraid of these Norwegians, the way Pat, here, would be sorry for him, and tell him where the *San Sebastian* is hidden – "

"Ssh!" Joe Fahy ran over and shut the kitchen door, shoving outside a few curious ducks who had followed us in. "No names, no pack-drill," he said over his shoulder to Ned.

I said:

"If you saw Manuel, Ned, you'd know he wasn't pretending to be afraid. I felt his arm shake under my hand. And when Erik called to him to come out, he was nearly crying with fright. I'm quite sure he was no friend of theirs tonight, though he may have been at one time."

"I wonder if they took him away to ask him questions. If they frightened him enough, perhaps he'll tell them that we hid the brig."

Bartley explained to the men that Manuel had overheard us talking about the brig.

"And now the whalers know it is hereabouts too," he said. "It was a pity you threw that bean-tin overboard, Pat."

"They may think it was Manuel threw the tin overboard," I said. "They only know the brig came this way. They don't know we had anything to do with it."

And I explained my theory that Manuel was so anxious to have the brig all to himself that he would keep his own counsel and hope that he would be able to escape and come back to fetch her.

"There's one thing certain sure," said Bartley.

"Manuel is not the rightful owner of the brig, and I'll go bail the whalers don't own her either. There is no time to be lost in seeing Mr Daly. If neither the whalers nor ourselves has the right to her, then we'll have to see about finding her real owner."

This was the first time I had ever heard Bartley allow that anyone could have a right to own wrack other than the man who brought it ashore. I could see that he was impressed at the lengths to which people were prepared to go to get possession of the brig, and he was beginning to think that the whole business was not as simple as it had seemed at first sight. He looked around the room now, and said:

"Well, we had better be getting back to tell herself what happened." I felt suddenly desolate until he went on: "You'll come too, Pat. You can't spend the night here alone."

He looked into my bedroom and remarked that the things had been thrown about there too. The big carved chest that had held my mother's wedding clothes was thrown open, and the blankets and linen that it had contained scattered about. A few old letters and papers lay in a little heap on the floor, as if someone had read through them. We left everything as it was. Bartley said:

"It's late enough now. We'll come back and tidy it up tomorrow, and I'll settle that door for you too."

We lifted the door into place and put a stone against it for security, and then with a last look backwards we started for Bartley's house.

The men were very excited about the whole affair. I could see by the way they still carried their weapons at the ready that they did not believe we had seen the last of the intruders. They kept their voices low, and as we crossed the fields they kept a sharp eye open for an ambush.

I did not expect that we would be molested. Mrs Folan had said that the whalers had gone to consult their chief. Now I felt sure that they had delivered Manuel to that same chief, and that they were finished with us for the time being. In the confusion it had been hard to guess which direction the horse and trap had taken. Talking it over now, we concluded that they had gone on the main road to the east. They would not have had to pass though the village that way, because Farran village is on a short road that runs off the main road and ends at the quay. It was likely that the chief was in hiding somewhere there along the coast. I thought it likely that they would hustle Manuel on to the trawler that Tomsy Fahy had seen, and take him away to one of the islands where the whalers were accustomed to put in, or even away to a Spanish port.

When we reached Bartley's house, Mrs Folan was standing at the kitchen door. She said nothing, but ran in before us and stood looking at us, with a hundred questions in her eyes. In as few words as possible, Bartley told her the story. She was furious about the broken china. As near as I could make out, she would have preferred it if we had found Manuel himself in as many pieces on the floor.

Suddenly she stopped lamenting and said:

"That's thirsty work you've all been at. Sit down now and I'll see have I any drop of the crayther for you."

She had, and a few minutes later all the visitors were smacking their lips over brimming glasses of poteen. There were not enough glasses to go round and some of them had to have mugs. The people who had these were very pleased, because they held more than the glasses. I had a mug of buttermilk, and she poured herself some deadly-looking strong tea from the pot that was still stewing on a broken turf-sod on the hearth.

It was after midnight when the men got up to go home. They stood up slowly, and you could see by their faces that they had not had half enough talk about the evening's work. Bartley saw them to the door, and thanked each one of them for his part.

"I'm glad we didn't come on those unfortunate whalers sooner," he said with a grin. "They'd have thought we were mistaking them for a field of spuds."

Whey they had all gone he came back and helped to make up a bed for me in the kitchen. I was so tired by now that I thought I could see two Bartleys stumping about the room. He waited until I was in bed, and then he said:

"I'll leave the room door open. If you hear a noise in the night, one shout will bring me running."

I looked up at him bleary-eyed, hardly knowing what he was saying. If a herd of elephants had charged through that kitchen during the night, I do not believe I should have heard them. I slept as if I were the man who invented sleep, and ran for my life in my dreams from unnamed terrors.

All the same, it was the quiet chuckle of a hen standing on the edge of the settle-bed that woke me in the morning.

6

I Set Out for Galway

I lay back in bed with my hands behind my head, looking out through the open door into the sunlight. The hen cocked her head on one side as if she were wondering if I would make a palatable bite. Then Mrs Folan crossed before the door carrying a dish of oats and calling out:

"*Chook*-chook-chook-chook-chook!"

My visitor jumped delicately on to the floor and galloped outside.

I stretched lazily. It was good to wake up to such pleasant everyday things. Now I could hardly believe in the face at the window and the gunshot and the plunging horse that had carried Manuel away. I wondered where he was now, and if he had slept as soundly as I had. I hoped he was not being badly used by the whalers, but with all my heart I prayed that I would never lay eyes on him again.

The old, hoarse-throated clock above my head struck nine. I had never been so late in bed before. I bounded up, but just then Mrs Folan came into the kitchen. She would not let me move until I had eaten a huge breakfast of eggs and soda-bread and butter, and had drunk several cups of strong tea. Then she said:

"There isn't sight nor light of the strangers this morning. Bartley was over to Farran early, and everyone says they're gone out of the district altogether."

"Small loss," said I. "I hope they won't be back."

"You never know," she said. "I'd say we won't see them for a few days anyway. Matt Faherty told Bartley this morning that one of them – a fair-haired fellow with yellow eyes like a goat – that he bought a piece of rope from him yesterday. He walked into the shop as cool as you please, and asked for a strong piece of rope, long enough to tie up a man with. Matt thought he was joking."

At that moment Bartley came in from outside, and said to me:

"Have you slept enough, Pat? I thought we'd have to duck you in the sea to wake you up."

"No wonder he'd sleep," said Mrs Folan. "Didn't I put a dropeen of the craythur into his buttermilk last night!"

That started an argument that was likely to last all day, by the sound of it. Bartley said I would be getting bad habits, and his wife said the poteen never did anyone any harm. Then Bartley began to tell stories of the awful consequences of drinking it too young, until I broke in:

"If it was poteen that gave me the nightmares last night, I'll never again have anything to do with it."

"Didn't it give you a fine night's sleep?" she protested. "Bartley and I ate our breakfast at the table beyond, and there wasn't a stir out of you."

"It gave me nightmares," I said firmly, "and it made me sleep so soundly that I could not wake myself up."

Bartley was delighted with this judgement. He put an end to the subject by asking me if I would like to go and visit the brig. This was exactly what I wanted, but as I jumped out of bed and began to dress I said:

"Perhaps we should not go near her, in case the whalers would see us."

"They're not about at all, I'm telling you," said Bartley. "Later on you can take the pony and ride in to Galway."

When we stepped outside I saw that it was another beautiful clear morning. There was a light breeze, however, which ruffled the sea and broke the tops of the little waves as they reached the shore. When we got the currach afloat, it moved about restlessly like a horse, until our weight quieted it down. As we pulled slowly out from the shore, Bartley said:

"There was a man from Galway below in Farran this morning, and he told me the whalers were in Achill last week. They had nine whales tied to the quay there, he said, floating because they had gone bad. He said you could smell them miles away."

"Are they in Achill still?"

"No. They are in Inishkee now. A ship came in and took away the whales, and then the men moved back to Inishkee. They have a trawler for going around after the whales, he said."

"That sounds like our Norwegians."

"It does so. This man said they are a bad lot. He didn't think they were real whalers at all. He said the people up that way never saw them before. And they didn't act like the whalers that usually come. They stole chickens and ducks and lambs off the mountainside. They're a bad lot, he said."

We rowed out to sea first, and then we turned to the west, until we came almost opposite the cave. We looked about carefully, both on land and sea, in case we were being watched. Bartley had a fishing-line in his pocket and he let it down and fished innocently for a few minutes. There was no sign of life anywhere about us, but we were taking no chances. Presently a rock-fish bit on the hook. Bartley hauled him aboard, unhooked him and flipped him back into the sea. Then he let down the line again. A few minutes later he felt another bite. When he pulled in the line, there was the same rock-fish for the second time.

"Look here, boy," said Bartley to the fish as he loosed him from the hook, "some people never learn from experience. I'll make you a present of the worm if you'll keep out of my boat."

He presented the surprised fish with the bait, and remarked to me:

"I'd scruple to eat such a fool of a fish."

We pulled in close and edged along under the cliffs. It was dark with shadow here, and we knew we were well out of sight. We made no splash with our oars, but dipped them carefully. In a moment we reached the cave mouth, and we shipped the oars and pushed ourselves inside with our hands on the cold walls.

There was just room for the currach at the side of the brig. Indeed, with the little sway of the waves, there was a danger that she would crush the currach against the cave wall. We got up to the bows as quickly as we could, and there we were out of danger. A dim light came through the puffing-holes in the roof of the cave, enough to see by but no more. We kept our voices low, lest anyone walking on the cliff above might hear us.

The tall side of the *San Sebastian* rose above us, and we looked up into the face of the figurehead under the bowsprit. Then I stepped on to the rope ladder that we had left hanging there and climbed aboard.

Bartley followed me and whispered:

"I want to go below. I haven't been through the hold properly yet."

Between the wheelhouse and the hatch that led to the lower deck, there was another hatch, much bigger, and obviously meant for cargo. We went down a rough ladder and found ourselves in pitch darkness. I had not been here at all, because I had been so busy showing the men the cabins and the crew's quarters and the galley.

"There are portholes," said Bartley, "but they are small, and now they are too near the walls of the cave to let in any light."

He had a candle-end in his pocket, and he lit it and held it aloft. Now we could see down the whole length of the hold. At first sight it was quite bare. The deck under our feet was dark with age, but clean. I remembered what Manuel had said, that the *San Sebastian* had always carried clean cargoes, of silver and copper and walnuts. But I could see that it was many years since the last cargo had lain here.

"There must be ballast under the deck," said Bartley. "I wonder what they used at the time when this ship was built."

I walked down towards the bows. Suddenly I said:

"Look there! Look there!"

Lying against the side was a single gold piece. Bartley stooped and picked it up, and we examined it together.

"It's the same as the ones that Manuel offered to me," I said. "It's the queerest looking money I ever saw. Where in the world did it come from?"

"Dropped out of Manuel's pocket," said Bartley. "Not so loud, Pat. Someone will hear you."

I whispered:

"Why did he drop it here? Doesn't it look as if he had a lot of it in here and some of it was forgotten?"

"People don't have sacks of gold nowadays," said Bartley. He turned the gold piece over and over in his fingers. "And still, that piece of money is a queer old age, I'm thinking. I'd like to see Matt Faherty's face if I offered it for a couple of ounces of tobacco in the shop."

He dropped it into his pocket.

"What will you do with it?" I asked.

"I'll keep it out of sight until Mr Daly sees it," said Bartley. "This is a strange business, Pat. I'm getting very uneasy about it all."

Round about on the deck where we were standing there were heavy drops of tallow that had fallen off a candle.

"Perhaps Manuel counted his money in here," I said. "You can see that he had a candle in here for a long time while he worked at something. Maybe he robbed a bank and escaped in the brig with the gold."

"What bank would have gold pieces like that?" said Bartley. "Besides, why would he use an ancient sailing-ship to escape in when he had a motor trawler?"

I could not answer that one, except to say that the trawler belonged to the Norwegians.

"And Manuel said he was no sailor," said Bartley. "I wonder where Chile comes into the story. I'm sure the brig herself is important, and she was not merely being used as a ship."

"If she could talk," said I, "we'd hear an odd story."

To me she seemed so very much a personality that I do not believe it would have surprised me to hear her laugh. It would be a soft, deep laugh, with a hundred harmonious notes blended together in it. Bartley recalled me to my senses.

"Up to the forecastle," he said. "I want to have a look at those blankets."

I followed him up on deck and then down the companion ladder in the stern to the crew's quarters. There was more light there, for now we were nearer to the mouth of the cave, and the portholes around the stern let in the daylight. We brought one of the old brown blankets to the light and looked it over carefully. It was heavy and coarse, and looked to us, who were accustomed to such things, to have been spun and woven by hand.

"These seem to me to be the blankets that were put into the ship the first day she was launched," said Bartley.

"But how could that be?" I objected. "The first blankets must have been worn out by the sailors on the voyages across the Atlantic many, many years ago."

"We only have Manuel's word for it that she sailed the Atlantic," said Bartley. He looked around. "The more I see of this ship, the more I think she never

did an honest day's work in her life. I think she was
built for show!"

Now, I did not like to hear this verdict, as you
may imagine. If she were only built for show, she
could hardly be called a real ship at all. I preferred to
think of her proudly sailing the high seas, riding the
gales and weathering the storms with her head held
high, and landing her precious cargo safely at the end
without mishap. And still I could not deny that what
Bartley had said had a sound of truth about it. She
was as well tended as a naval ship in port, as if she
was always expecting visitors. Of course I knew that
this was the way a ship should be, but I also knew
that few achieve it. I wondered if Manuel and the
whalers had stolen her from a marine museum. I had
never heard that the like existed, but I supposed that
it was possible.

Bartley said:

"I think there was once some kind of a label
stitched on to this blanket. Look here at the corner."

Someone had removed the label unskillfully,
leaving brown threads hanging.

"There was probably a name and address on it," I
said. "It may have been taken off to make it harder to
find the owner of the brig."

"Look at the other blankets," said Bartley.

We examined them all, and on each we found
traces of a recently removed label.

"Someone went to a great deal of trouble," said
Bartley at last.

"Manuel would never have thought of cutting off the labels," said I, " and there are no other marks to show who is the owner."

We went up to the cabins on deck, but though we searched everywhere here too, we found nothing.

"I think they did not use these cabins at all," said Bartley. "They probably felt more at home below."

Before we left the brig, we stood on deck and looked up at the high vaulted roof of the cave above our heads. The mainmast almost reached to the top. We could not see the sea from where we stood, for an outcropping rock at the cave mouth just cut it off from our view.

"But for this cave we could never have hidden her," said Bartley. "There's caves like it in the Aran Islands too. I saw them once."

"If the sea gets rough, she'll smash her mast on the roof," I said, and Bartley answered:

"She'll smash up altogether if the sea gets rough. I won't be easy until she's out of this."

We climbed down the ladder into the currach, and before we left the cave we made sure that the *San Sebastian* was still moored securely to her rock. Then we edged our way out into the open. We paused in the mouth of the cave, with the black prow of the currach invisible against the black cliff wall, while we made sure that no one was watching us. Then we slipped outside, and a few quick strokes of the oars sent us shooting away to a safe distance. We made no pretence of fishing this time, but set out for home at once.

It was almost noon by the time we had the currach ashore and were on our way up to the house. Perhaps I felt a premonition of approaching disaster, for I can still remember how it seemed to me that the little sloe bushes were crouching low against the ground and the heads of the wild flowers hidden in terror in the grass. I would not for the world have mentioned this fancy to Bartley, but I kept very close to his bent figure as we climbed upwards.

At the house, too, there was an air of hurry. Mrs Folan had our dinner ready, and while we ate we told her about our visit to the brig and the finding of the gold piece.

"I don't like that," she said. "I'd like to hear the rest of the story of that ship. Eat up, now, Pat. There's no time to be lost."

Before I had finished, Bartley got up and went out. I heard him climb the stile into the next field to catch the pony, and then the rattle of the bridle as he slipped it over his head. As I swallowed the last bite he led the pony around to the door. He threw the reins over the hitching post and came inside.

"When you get to Galway, go straight to Michael Daly's office," he said. He fumbled in his pocket and took out an envelope. "Give him this letter and let him read it before you tell him your story. Leave nothing out – tell him about the gold piece, and about Manuel, and about the Norwegians prowling about the house. Tell him about the labels being cut off the blankets. Tell him exactly what the brig looks like, and where we have her hidden."

"Will I tell him that too?"

"Yes, of course. You can trust Mr Daly. He will know what to do. Say we must have help at once, because the brig should be brought into Galway where she will be safe. Will you remember all that?"

"I'll remember," I said.

Mrs Folan filled my pockets with soda-cake and promised to feed my ducks in the evening.

"You'll be back before dark," she said. "Take the pony into Fogarty's yard in Galway and they'll give him a feed of oats."

I went out and climbed into the saddle. Bartley tightened the girth, while the pony twitched his ears and shifted his feet impatiently. I patted his neck and he shook his mane at me.

"Faith then you'll be the tired pony this evening," said Mrs Folan as she rubbed his nose. "You're in a great hurry to be off."

For the first time in her life she gave me no messages to do in Galway. I promised myself that I would buy her a china bowl with roses on it, which she had admired on the last market-day.

Bartley held the bridle for a moment longer as he said:

"Don't delay in Galway, Pat. You can hurry on the road in, and start back at about five o'clock. I wish I was going with you." He let go the bridle and said: "I'll be mending the door while you're gone!"

I started off then, and at the turn into the boreen I looked back. There were the two of them, side by side, still watching me. Suddenly they looked small and old, and I felt that the burden of the whole business had settled down on me.

However, I could not be depressed for long on such a beautiful day. It was only one o'clock, and the sun was high overhead. The pony picked his way carefully among the stones of the boreen. He was a real Connemara pony, silver-grey, with small ears, sensitive mouth and the arched neck of his Arab ancestors. He was completely at ease with my weight on his back and it pleased me greatly to fall in with his every movement. When we reached the main road, I trotted him over to the wide grassy margin, and then I made him fly along in a canter, like a silver arrow. His long tail flew out behind us, and I straightened my legs in the stirrups and sat firmly in the saddle so as not to retard him. I wondered how long he would be able to keep up this pace. There were seventeen miles of road between us and Galway, and even the best horse would begin to flag before the end of such a journey. At present he looked as if he could go on all day. I guessed that he enjoyed it all the more because most of his time was spent under the cart.

In the houses we passed, the people had come in for their midday meal. Now the men came to the doors and waved their caps to me as I passed. At Farran crossroad I saw Ned Donnelly riding down

Mc Connell

towards the village. He turned in the saddle and
shouted to me, and his horse whinnied to mine. I
knew that within ten minutes the whole village
would know that Pat Hernon was on his way into
Galway on Bartley's pony.

A mile or two beyond Farran the houses were less
frequent. The road ran down to the level of the sea
here, and barren fields of rock stretched away on my
right hand as far as the shore. On my left was the
Carnan mountain, rising directly above the road.
Outcropping rocks hung over my head as I passed.
No one lived on the mountain, for it was all marsh
and bog and rocks. In the higher parts of it there
were deep, cold bog-lakes with brown water, ringed
with reeds. I had often fished for trout there, on
holidays.

Presently the road mounted, until it crossed over
the shoulder of the mountain. The pony slowed to a
trot now, against the hill. I hoped I had not let him
get overheated, and I was glad that he would have to
move more slowly for a while. At the highest point of
the road I stopped for a moment and looked down at
the glittering sea. Then, still keeping the pony on the
grassy edge, I started down the hill. It was very steep,
and the going was slow. However, I knew that after
this we would have no trouble. We were six miles
from home already.

The pony's hooves made only the smallest
whispering sound on the soft grass. There were prints
of another horse's hooves here, and I wondered who

had been along this way already. I thought I would catch sight of him soon, for when I would have rounded the next bend I would be looking along the straight road to Galway. I shook the reins at the idea of this, for I thought it would be pleasant to have company for the remainder of the journey.

At the bend of the road there was a huge grass-grown rock which completely cut off the view of the road ahead. I reached the point of the turn, and then, before I knew what I was doing, I reined the pony hard.

Standing at the other side of the rock, there was a little group of men. None of them spoke. One stood in front of the others, and I looked into the still, cold depths of his evil eyes for the longest moment in the world. They were the eyes of a snake, or of some strange underwater fish. I knew that face well. It was the face I had seen at the window.

The pony gave a long shiver that brought me to myself. I shouted wildly, and kicked at his flanks with my heels. He sprang forward. The group came to life. One of them seized the bridle. Another caught at my leg and pulled me to the ground. I remember calling myself a fool for not having spurred on the pony when I first saw the men, instead of pulling up and letting myself fall into their hands. Even while I kicked and fought my captors, I shouted to the pony to get away. He wrenched his bridle free. Up came his front hooves, sending the men sprawling back on top of each other in fear. Then with a long wild whinny he whirled around, iron shoes drumming on stone, tail and mane flying, and flashed back along the road we had come.

The men crowded to watch him go, and hurled evil wishes after him. They used their own language, which I did not understand, but there was no mistaking the tone of their voices. From the bitter looks they threw to each other, I guessed that each was blaming the rest for the pony's escape. It was some satisfaction to me to know that they had not meant this to happen. They probably realised that when the riderless pony would return to Bartley's house, the hue and cry would be out after me at once. Then it occurred to me that this might not be such a good thing. If they felt secure they would do nothing desperate, but if they felt that they were pursued they might decide to dump me in a bog-hole and pretend that they had never heard of me.

These thoughts did not proceed through my mind in as orderly a fashion as I write them down. Held in the grip of one of the men, a bow-legged, monkey-faced, steel-fisted desperado, no doubt my eyes stared with fright and my mouth hung open, and I am certain that tears of rage stained my face. I turned desperately to look down the road, but there was no one in sight. We stood in the middle of the road, where the men had dragged me to watch the pony gallop up the hill. No one was coming that way either. I knew it was no use shouting, for no one lived hereabouts. A cold despair settled down on me.

The man whom Manuel had called Erik Vilifson seemed to be the leader. Now he issued a command in a venomous whisper. The men fell silent at once. The one who was holding me gave me a vicious jerk forward. Still he held my wrist so that I thought he wanted to break off my hand and have it for himself. The others closed in around us, five of them altogether. Then they struck off up the mountain by a tiny track, bringing me with them, at a brisk march.

7

Juan

That was an extraordinary journey. We followed the little track for miles, upward and along the side of the mountain. We saw no movement of life up there, except a few sheep, and once a lost lamb that followed us, bleating, until one of the men chased it away. They never spoke. After I had got over my first terror, I tried to make them tell me where we were going. My second question shrivelled up and died when Erik whipped out a knife from nowhere and said in a husky snarl:

"If you speak, I cut your throat!"

There was no doubt that he meant it. Somehow I lost all desire to find out our destination.

Presently my legs became very weary. I was barefoot, of course, so I should have been comfortable enough, but the men set such a pace that my bones ached all over after a few miles. Away on all sides stretched the wide grey-green bog, untouched, untravelled by man for many a year. The path had faded away, but still they steered their way through the apparently trackless country with confidence. One of the men carried a small compass and this seemed to be all they needed. The part we were in was known as a quaking bog, and had the reputation of being able to swallow a man without a trace. I marvelled at their coolness, until it occurred to me that they had never heard of its dangers. From then on, my heart was in my mouth at every step. As the hours passed and the sun sailed unconcerned across the sky, I thought they would at least stop for a bite to eat. But they were above such things, it seemed. Once I put my hand to my pocket, thinking that I would nibble some of Mrs Folan's soda-bread. My keeper gave a sideways chop at my wrist with the heel of his fist, and my hand fell paralysed at my side.

They had not searched me, and I thought this was a strange thing. It must be that none of these black-avised villains was the chief, for surely he would have thought of such an elementary thing. This thought made me breathe more freely. Until now I had not known at what moment I would feel a knife in my back.

Next I got to thinking about the pony, and how he must have reached home by now. I knew he would to straight to Bartley for comfort, but I could imagine that Bartley would have little time to spare for him when he would find that I was missing. I wondered what he would do. I could imagine him summoning all his friends from Farran first, and then searching the long road into Galway lest the pony had thrown me and I was lying somewhere injured. After that, what could they do? It was too much to hope that they would catch up on the whalers and rescue me before there was time to get me out of reach.

Late in the afternoon we crossed the highest point of the mountain. The wind whined though the rough grass there, and whistled mournfully past my ears like a dying banshee. The last drop of my courage ran out. It seemed to me that I was doomed to walk on this mountain for the rest of my living days, never getting anywhere but always moving onward. Then we began to descend the slope on the other side. I looked away down on my left, and saw fold on fold of grey-brown mountain and valley, scarred with white limestone and pitted with slate-coloured lakes. Down through the valleys a sandy road wove in and out, the first road I had seen since my capture. Unreasonably, I felt cheered at the sight of the road. It was at least a sign that we had not gone into a different world. It was a wild and desolate scene, however, with not a house, nor a tree, nor any sign of the existence of man except the twisting white road.

We did not walk on the road, but kept to the grass at the side. Turf had been cut here once, long ago, and Erik said, breaking the long silence in his careful English:

"If I tell you, you lie down."

I supposed that if anyone happened to come this way, we would climb into the ditch and lie motionless until they had passed. No one would see us unless they were looking for us.

But there was no need to hide. In the turf-cutting season we would have met people, but it was too early in the year for that. Each time we rounded a bend or an outcropping rock I hoped that I would find my rescuers on the other side, but at last I came to the bitter conclusion that every man in this part of Connemara must be in an enchanted sleep.

As evening fell, a great stillness came over the huge mountains. Rabbits came out to play and watched us from a safe distance. A big brown hare squatted on his hunkers, boldly staring. At another place a fox sloped off, looking back over his shoulder, his white front gleaming. Great black shadows drifted across the sky. The sun went down out of sight behind us, and a small, cold night-wind began to blow. Still in the dimness my captors marched purposefully on, as if they did not even see the desolation and terrible lonesomeness all around us. Once night had fallen I gave up hoping for a chance rescue, for the Connemara men avoided such roads as this after dark.

I do not know what they would have done if it had been a pitch-dark night. They would not have dared to show a light, and without one they would not have been able to keep to the road. However, a thin moon came from behind the clouds, and we were just able to see the grey line of the road ahead of us.

After dark, I lost all account of time. I almost dozed as I walked. After we reached the road, we seemed to keep to the top of the mountain for a while. Then very gradually we were moving downhill. This made the going a little easier, until Erik made us quicken our pace. The men growled a little among themselves at that, and I was sourly pleased at the first sign of humanity among them. Erik himself seemed to be tireless, and he kept his place at the front all the time.

We went downhill for so long that I guessed we were making for the other road into Galway, the road that runs along by Lough Corrib and the river. It looked as if they were taking me into Galway after all, and I could not imagine why they should do this. I would have thought they would avoid the town, lest some inquisitive citizen ask them a question. Then I remembered how they had not feared to stand in a threatening band on the roadside to capture me, nor had they feared to prowl about my house uttering threats. I began to fear that the most inquisitive citizen that ever was would take one look at those devilish faces and curb his curiosity to save his life.

Presently the road widened and the surface became smoother. Then we passed a sleeping house or two, sheltered behind rose bushes and hay-barns. Walled fields appeared on either side, instead of the bog, and in the silence I heard more than once the heavy breathing of cows. Then at last we came to a crossroads.

Our sandy road ended here, at the main road into Galway. There was a wide grassy space at the cross, with small trees. My foot knocked against a clipping of tin that flashed for a second in the moonlight, so that I guessed this to be a common camping-ground for tinkers. We moved in under the trees and paused at last. Erik went forward alone, and became one with the darkness. One of the men moved over to my other side and gripped my arm, to make sure I would not escape, I suppose. He could have saved himself the trouble. I could not even have thought about escape then, I was so weary. In a moment Erik was back, leading a horse that towered above his head. The horse moved almost without a sound, so that I guessed he wore duffle shoes. I had heard of these, though I had never seen them. Now I saw that he was harnessed to a trap. I wondered if this were the same horse and trap that had carried off Manuel only last night. I remember wondering how the horse liked being forced into taking part in such crimes. Then, as Erik turned him around, I saw in a flash of moonlight his savage eye and bared teeth, and I decided that if there were such things as criminal horses, this must be one.

Now I found myself being forced into the trap. It was a big one, deep and wide. I was pushed to the front, and the man who had held me all the time got in beside me. I had not been separated by as much as a foot from that man all day, and I had come to dislike him heartily. Another man held the horse's head, and Erik got in opposite me and took the reins. Then a third man, of the group that had escorted me over the mountain, took the last place beside Erik, and the trap was full. This meant that two of the men were not coming with us. I guessed that there must be at least one other man there in the darkness under the trees, who had brought the horse to meet us.

Erik shook the reins and the big horse moved forward. The wheels of the trap were rubber-tyred, and the duffle-shoes made only a soft pad-pad on the road. The road was overhung with trees for a good part of the way, unlike our bleak road by the sea. We kept to the side, and the horse settled down to a steady trot. Through gaps in the trees I got occasional glimpses of Lough Corrib away down on my left. The moon made it glitter brightly against the dark landscape.

Suddenly I felt faint and sick with hunger. I had been too tired to think of food for a long time, but now that the life was coming back into my limbs, food became the next urgent need. I used up my last drop of courage to say:

"Erik, I'm hungry!"

Then, before he could tell me to hold my tongue, I went on:

"I won't be much use to the chief if I die of hunger."

I was a long way from dying, for I had often fasted for hours on a day's fishing. But I could feel that Erik was turning over the idea I had put into his mind, and I hoped he was puzzled to know what to do. His own inclination would be to let me die if I pleased, but I fancied that his chief wanted me alive. He growled:

"I have no food for you. Do you think this is a grocer's shop?"

"I have food here in my pocket," I said. "I brought it from home. If you will tell your watch-dog not to bite, I'll take it out and eat it."

"Very well."

He muttered something to my guard. The food was in my left-hand pocket, on the side away from him. I slipped my hand into my pocket and took out the little parcel. Before I did so, my fingers closed on the envelope containing Michael Daly's letter from Bartley.

I had forgotten all about it. I did not know how much Bartley had said in the letter. Perhaps he had even mentioned where the brig was hidden. It would not be like Bartley to take the risk of naming the place, but he had been so certain that I would deliver the letter into Mr Daly's hands that I thought he might have done so.

I opened the packet of sandwiches and took one out. It was beautifully soft, and I could feel with my finger-tips that there were sultanas in the bread. I did not offer any to the men, for I had no evidence that they had acquired the habit of eating. I took a heavenly bite and munched.

As I ate, I felt my courage slowly seeping back. I

began to think about the letter again, and to plan what I was going to do with it. Of course, I could not risk its falling into the hand of the enemy. If they did get it, and if it contained the information they sought, it would probably cost me my life. I had realised that as long as I kept my own counsel I was safe, but that when I would have passed on my information for a promise of freedom, there would be an end of me. How could these scoundrels roam the world after they would have got the brig, knowing that I was alive to describe their black deeds and their villainous faces? I had been remarkably lucky until now, in that they had not searched me. I was sure that this state of things could not continue for long.

The best thing, then, would be to get rid of the letter before I was brought before the chief. At this moment I could have dropped it out of the trap on to the road without being seen. It seemed to me that it would be better if I could manage to drop it in Galway, where someone would perhaps find it and deliver it to Mr Daly. Bartley had written his name and address on the outside.

I was now convinced that I was being brought to Galway. We were passing though a populous district, where a group of foreigners could not have a hiding-place unnoticed. But in Galway there would be boats, and queer empty warehouses down by the docks that would provide plenty of cover. If the letter were found in Galway, I thought, Bartley would have a sign that I had passed that way.

So we travelled on along the hilly road through the dark country. We carried no light, and we passed no lighted houses on the way until we came to the outskirts of Galway. From then on there was an occasional street lamp which only made the darkness in between all the more dense. We padded down between the silent houses, and turned to the left. We crossed the wooden canal bridge, and later the big stone bridge over the salmon weir. Then we rounded the Court House and started down the broad street by the Guard's barracks. This was exactly what I had hoped for. We were going to pass Mr Daly's very door.

I had kept one sandwich until now so that I would have an excuse for dipping my hand in my pocket again. When I took out the sandwich I brought the letter with it. The men did not notice, for they were busily scanning the street for possible observers. I let my hand trail over the side of the trap, just as we passed Mr Daly's office, and the letter tumbled down on to the road. The wheels of the trap just cleared it, for which I was thankful. If it looked dirty and old it might perhaps lie there for a week, unless the street cleaners swept it away. I looked back and saw it shining white under the street lamp.

We were approaching the Guards' barracks now, and all the men were anxiously watching for the shine of silver buttons. A light showed downstairs, but no Guard came out. Then we had passed, and my last hope of rescue was gone. A minute later we were in back streets on our way to the docks.

I had often been at the Galway docks before. When Bartley and I came in to the market, we never missed paying a visit here. There would often be Connemara sailing-boats tied up against the quay wall, pookawns and nobbies that had sailed in with loads of turf or beasts for sale. The Claddagh men were always to be found at their own part of the docks, pottering about in their boats, and ready to stop and chat with a visitor at any time. Soon I saw that we were going to avoid the more populous parts. We passed down by the Aran Island steamer and the pilot-boat, and out on to a long windy deserted pier. Down at the end of it was the lay-by, where boats were hauled up for painting and repairs. There were a few yachts moored there. Since there were no houses near it was all very quiet.

Erik drove the trap all down the length of the pier. As we neared the end, a man slipped off a bollard where he had been sitting and disappeared, I supposed, down a ladder against the quay wall. At the spot where the man had disappeared, Erik reined in the horse. While my watch-dog still held me fast, the third man opened the door, got down and went around to the horse's head. Then Erik hissed at me:

"Get out! Quiet!"

I was jerked out on to the quay.

"Over the side!" said Erik, still in a hissing whisper.

Suddenly I could not bear to climb tamely down that ladder into my captors' boat. I remembered a schoolboy trick that I had been good at once. I hooked one bare foot around my watch-dog's ankle, and had the satisfaction of seeing him crash to the ground. Unfortunately he held on to me until he hit the ground, so that I almost went down with him. When he let go, I staggered back a pace or two. Thus I lost the one moment's start I should have had, while the other two were still surprised. By the time they had recovered I should have been halfway up the quay, running like a hare.

But it did not work out like that. I had not taken two steps when Erik's iron hand was fixed into the back of my collar like the hook of a crane. I kicked at him wildly, but I might have saved myself the trouble, for all the impression my bare toes made on his shins. His left hand shot out and crashed into my jaw, so that my brains jangled together. I could do nothing whatever to save myself from then on, though I was more or less aware of what was happening to me.

The watch-dog was off the ground now, snarling. I took it that he was for adding a punch or two of his own, but Erik restrained him. He swung my helpless body over his shoulder as if it had been a sack of potatoes and started down the ladder with me. I wanted to bite and kick, but I had no breath for either exercise. I only knew that at the foot of the ladder I was dumped on the deck of a small ship, before I went completely unconscious.

When I came to myself the ship was moving, as I knew by the beat of her engines and her gentle swing with the sea. I was lying on a bunk somewhere below decks. I felt mighty sorry for myself for having been so rudely used, but I knew I could not have been unconscious for long, because I could see through the portholes that it was still night. If there had been any doubt as to whether I would remember what had happened, the ache in my jaw and the dried blood on my face would have reminded me.

The bunk where I lay was in a tiny cabin, lit by an oil lamp that swung with the motion of the boat. I guessed that I was in a small trawler, possibly the very one that I had seen yesterday. The cabin was clean, but besides another bunk above my head, the only other furniture was a chair.

I sat up cautiously and swung my legs on to the floor, with my head swimming. I stood up, and walked a step, unsteadily enough. I went over to the one porthole, to see if it were big enough for me to get through. It was not. Of course, they would not have left me here if I could have climbed out so easily. I did not ask myself what I would have done if I could have got out, for I had not considered that question yet.

Suddenly I seized the chair by the back and swung it above my head, missing the lamp by an inch. In another moment I would have sent it smashing against the cabin door, had not a quiet voice said:

"Put down that chair."

I felt a horrid prickling of the skin. The chair dropped from my hands. I sank back against the door and looked upwards. Lying on one elbow in the upper bunk, regarding me quietly, was a man. I had never seen him before. We stared at each other for a long moment. He had penetrating grey eyes and a calculating, half-humorous expression. He was black-haired and sunburned, like Manuel, and his long-fingered, quiet hands, folded in front of him, were olive-brown. At last he said:

"You are Pat Hernon. I heard them talking about you. Hernon – that is like a Spanish name."

"I am not a Spaniard," I said sharply.

He laughed, a low silky chuckle.

"I have never known a Spaniard called Pat," he said. Then he went on quickly, as if he feared that he had offended me: "I am a Spaniard. My name is Juan de Toro. I am a prisoner here, like you."

"Why?" I asked quickly.

He shrugged.

"It's a long story. It concerns a brig called the *San Sebastian*."

I looked at him quickly, but he seemed to be not observing me. He pointed to the chair.

"If you had smashed that chair against the door, you might have brought them all in on top of us. There are four of them and only two of us."

"Where are they taking us? And why should they mind if I make a noise, since we are at sea?"

"That kind never likes a noise. As to where they

118

are taking us, I do not know. They make a great secret of that."

I seized the chair again.

"I'll smash down that door!" I shouted. "If it brings them all in, so much the better! At least I can argue it out with them then."

"No one argues with those fellows," said the other calmly. "The less we see of them the better."

"Well, Mr Juan de Toro, since you know so much about them, perhaps you can tell me why they have kidnapped me," said I bitterly, playing the injured innocent.

Juan sighed.

"They can think of only one thing," he said, "and that is a brig called the *San Sebastian*. I heard only a few words of what they said about you, but they seem to think that you know something about the brig, and could tell them if you wished."

He took out a short black cigar and lit it with precise movements. I asked:

"And do you know something about this brig?"

"Oh yes. I know all about it, except that I do not know where it is now. You see, I am the owner of the brig – or I was until our violent friends stole it and sailed away."

"*You* are the owner of the brig?"

"Why not?" He raised his eyebrows. "Why should I not own a brig?"

"Of course," I stammered, alarmed at how narrowly I had escaped giving myself away. "Tell me about it."

At first I thought he was not going to talk any more. He lay there looking at the ceiling and quietly puffing smoke. I watched him, holding my breath, wondering if I were going to hear the real story of the *San Sebastian* at last. Presently he began:

"Have you ever heard of a country called Chile?"

"Yes," I said. "I know a good deal about Chile."

"That is surprising. You must have been well taught your geography at school."

"And my history too," I said grimly.

"Then doubtless you will remember that at the time of the Chilean revolution, the Spanish governor was called Mateo de Toro?" As I made no answer he went on: "Mateo was my great-great-grand-uncle. He had the *San Sebastian* built in Valparaiso, and when the revolution began, he sailed back to Spain in her, in 1810. He traded a little with the brig, but most of the time he just kept her anchored at Santander. That is why she is not worn out, like so many of her contemporaries. And because she looks so young, she is very valuable. A week ago she was stolen from Santander by Erik and his friends, who call themselves whalers. I followed them, but they captured me and held me prisoner. I have been taken to many places on this trawler, and I do not know what they intend to do with me at last."

It may be imagined with what confusion this story filled me. Juan spoke far better English than Manuel and seemed altogether a cleverer man. Surely, if one or other of them owned the brig, it must be Juan. His story was not as long-winded as Manuel's, but it had more of the sound of truth about it. I was by nature too cautious to tell the whole story of my finding of the brig on such short acquaintance, but I was very much tempted to do so. Juan's eyes were gentle and kind, and had none of the obvious, grasping eagerness that I had seen in Manuel. It was a lonesome thing to be trepanned and far from home, and it would have been a comfort to lean for help on someone else. But I could not help thinking that Bartley would not like it, that he would have advised me not to be in too much of a hurry, and that I had nothing to lose by waiting. After I moment I said:

"What do you think we should do?"

"Escape when we can," he said with a shrug. "Later on, we could start looking for the brig."

I was glad that he had not asked me directly to tell him what I knew of the brig's whereabouts, for I did not trust myself to refuse with sufficient certainty. Juan went on, in the same cool tone that he had used all the time:

"Of course, if I find that my life is in danger, I'll very soon resign my rights in the brig. It would not be very much use to me if I were dead."

He pulled gently at his cigar.

"How do you feel about it?" he asked, his eyes on the ceiling.

"I'm not as tame as you are," I said. "It would be a sore task to separate me from either my property or my life."

He looked at me quizzically.

"You're very fierce, for a young lad. But as you get older you will become more tolerant. You will be able to weigh the for and against, and you will find that the number of things for which you will risk your life will be very few."

"My friend, Bartley Folan, is sixty-five, and he is twice as fierce as I am," I said, and added contemptuously: "I would not have lived even as long as I have if I were as reasonable as you."

He flushed with anger, but after a short silence he said:

"Let us not fall out with each other. We have enough difficulties, even if we stand together."

I was beginning to regret having insulted him, and I might even have apologised if we had not at that moment heard a bolt drawn back on the outside of the door. Then the door opened and Erik stood looking at me with his cold snake's eyes. He did not look up at Juan at all. Behind him, I could see his three henchmen grouped, to prevent us from escaping, I supposed.

I did not feel like escaping. All my brave words to Juan would have sounded hollow enough now. The truth is that I was sadly frightened, so that I was pleased enough not to disgrace myself by begging to be released. My familiar enemies were the winds and the sea, and I was not afraid of them. But this cold-voiced person, so different from anyone I had ever met before, struck terror into me by his very strangeness. He explained that we were to make a two-days' voyage, at the end of which we would land at a small foreign port which he did not name. We were to be quiet, and to go ashore without calling for help, or Erik himself would make an end of us. It did not occur to me to doubt this, for he seemed so pleased at the prospect. He turned and went out. The other men stood watching, while one of them came forward with a can of greasy stew which he had been carrying. He laid it on the floor, and another put two tin plates and a little handful of cutlery beside it. Then they went out silently and the bolt slid into place again. I looked up at Juan, who had not spoken at all. The sight of the homely food brought a lump to my throat.

"I think we can safely eat the stew," said Juan. "We do not know when we will be offered food again."

So I poured the stew on to the plates, and we silently devoured half of it each. I had to hand Juan's up to him, for he seemed too indolent to descend, even for his food. It was a good stew, probably made from a stolen lamb, I thought, but none the less sweet for that. When we had finished, Juan said:

"Now we should sleep. We can do nothing until we land."

"Yes, but the moment we are ashore we should make a bolt for it," said I, having recovered a little of my courage with the stew.

But Juan would not agree to that. I pleaded that we could expect to be protected by the presence of loungers on the quay, but he insisted that it would be better to wait until we would be locked up somewhere, and escape quietly. That way, we would have a start on them. I could see that there was truth in this, though I hated the idea of seeming to be cowed. But Juan was a grown man, and likely to have better judgement that I had, and he seemed to know more about Erik and his friends than I did. Suddenly I remembered something.

"Bartley thought that Erik was not the leader," I said. "If we are being brought to the leader now, surely we will find it even harder to escape then than at the landing-port. Surely the leader will be cleverer than Erik and will give us no chance to escape."

"I think Bartley was wrong," said Juan. "I am sure that Erik is the leader."

Still I pointed out that if in our next prison we were confined separately, we would be in worse difficulties than ever. Juan was quite confident that we would be together, and at last I agreed that we would not make a disturbance on the quay.

I got into my bunk again and lay down. I had time only for a fleeting thought of Bartley, who must be searching the whole country for me, before I fell into a heavy, dreamless sleep.

The next day passed like an age. Hour after hour the blue sea hurried past the porthole. It seemed that night would never fall. We hardly spoke at all. Twice during the day, food was handed in to us, and once Juan was taken away for a while to be questioned.

He returned looking none the worse, and said casually that he had not parted with any information. They did not come for me, though I expected it momently. When at last it was night, it was hard to fall asleep. I lay awake for a long time, thinking of the *San Sebastian* and exploring every corner of her lovingly in my mind. It was the sound of the trawler's side grinding against a quay wall that woke me.

8

8

The House in the Rocks

I started broad awake. A greyness at the porthole told me that it was the dawn. I sprang off the bunk and went to look out. Our cabin was on the shore side, and I saw that we were lying against a short stone pier. A little distance away I could see the houses of a hilly town, with grey slate roofs and sloping gardens. I judged that it was no more than six o'clock, though there were a few people already about. I recognised one of our men busily tying the trawler's ropes to iron rings on the quay. Then Erik and another landed and walked up the pier towards the town. Juan still lay on his bunk, and I gave him a running account of all I could see. I wished I could look out on the sea side, because I wanted to know the nature of the coast on which we were, and whether we were in a bay. From the porthole I had only a shore view on either hand.

It was half an hour before Erik came back along. I

watched him step on board, and a moment later he swung open our cabin door. His two henchmen stood behind him.

"You come out now," he said, "and you do not speak."

I was surprised that he had not brought all his men with him, for he could not know that we had decided not to make a run for it. I was almost sorry now that we were not to risk an attempt at escape. There were three of them against two of us, which would have given us a sporting chance, I thought. However, it was too late now to change our minds, for I knew it would be no use trying it without consulting Juan.

We went out of the cabin in front of the men. They watched us closely while we stepped ashore, but they did not speak. Now I had my first real look at the trawler. Its name was painted on the bows in faded gold: *Santa Teresa*. A second trawler, which looked deserted, was moored behind ours. It was called *San Fernando,* and looked as if it had been built to match ours.

My legs shook at the knees, in spite of me. Juan seem quite unconcerned, and wore the same expression of half-humorous tolerance, as if he were rather bored with the whole business. I admired him for it, and did my best to copy him, but I did not think that I succeeded very well. Once we were on the quay the men closed in behind us. We passed several groups of people that I thought would notice the strangeness of our party, but they seemed too busy with their own concerns.

It was a tiny town, and it took only a few minutes to walk through its crooked main street. The houses were built of granite, and some of their doors already stood open directly on to the street. I glanced into one or two and saw big cool kitchens and white-capped women working. I wondered what country this could be. I thought it might be Spain, but then we did not seem to have come far enough. And the people did not look like Manuel. They were sunburned, to be sure, but they had neither the black hair nor the brooding brown eyes that Manuel had.

In a very short time we had left the town behind and were walking along a country road. There were high hedges on either side, so that I could not see into the fields. We passed one or two houses, each with a well for water outside the door. Some had home-made hutches with half a dozen rabbits cowering in each. I thought this very strange.

Knowing Erik's capacity for walking, I had no idea how far they were going to bring us. I noted each landmark as we passed – a church here, an orchard there, or a haybarn – so that I would know my way back. I hoped Juan was doing the same.

We walked along that road for perhaps an hour, and then we turned off into a laneway. This soon led us to the shore again, and we followed the coastline for about a mile. It was the most extraordinary coast I had ever seen. On the shore there were scattered immense granite rocks, as high as tall houses. Long reefs stretched out into the sea. Since the sun had come up the sea was a deep, clear blue, and dotted here and there for a long way there were more enormous rocks. Our road turned inland again for a piece, so that there were low cliffs between us and the sea. Then we turned a corner and came to a small fresh-water lake, with rushes growing around the rim. Across at the other side was the oddest little house I had ever seen. Someone had taken a fancy to build it between two huge boulders, with one gable against each. The boulders stuck up at either side above the roof-top, so that it looked as if the little house was held firmly down by the ears. Its door was painted white, and the white shutters closed over the windows looked like staring eyes. The rocky field in which it stood reminded me of home.

A path led around the lake to a gate of the field. Even at this distance I could see a small notice on the gate. As we came nearer I saw that it was in some strange language, not at all like the Spanish of the ship's papers.

"What is this place?" I asked Erik.

"Brittany," he said, and then he seemed to regret having answered. He looked quickly at Juan, and then said fiercely to me: "I tell you not to speak!"

"You cut my throat," said I before I could stop myself, and the next moment he nearly did.

For a long minute, while his yellow, goat's eyes looked into mine three inches away, I called myself a fool. His knife, pressed against my throat, seemed to thirst for my blood. The Juan said sharply:

"Put up that knife!"

To my astonishment, Erik put it away at once, with an almost apologetic air. I went around to the other side of my watch-dog, of whom I had suddenly become quite fond. I could not understand what had happened, but I was certain that Juan had saved my life.

After this little incident, the men opened the gate and hustled us over to the house. They had a key, and in a second the door was opened and we were inside in a cold little hallway. Two rooms opened off the hall, one on either side, and we were pushed without ceremony into the left-hand one. We heard the key turn in the lock.

The one window was shuttered, so that we were in a grey-black gloom. I made out the shapes of pieces of furniture, and I could feel a bare board floor under my feet. I whispered to Juan the question which I was longing to ask:

"Why did Erik put away his knife when you told him?"

I could not see him, but I could imagine Juan's shrug and a tolerant smile as he answered:

"If you give an order sharply enough, people will obey you."

I had heard that this was the way to deal with lions and tigers in the jungle, so I accepted the explanation.

"What will we do now?" I asked after a moment.

"We'll wait for a while," said Juan. "We must try to discover their plans first."

"Wouldn't it be better to escape at once?" I objected.

"And be followed and caught? No, no. That will not do. It will be much better to wait until they relax their guard a little, and then we will get away. Listen! Can you hear a man breathing, outside the door?"

We held our breath, and I heard it – the sound of a man standing very close to the door. Suddenly I said:

"Juan! There is someone in this room with us!"

"Nonsense," said Juan.

I clutched him and hissed:

"There is someone. I heard him move there in the silence. Strike a light, quickly!"

Without another word he struck a match and held it high above his head. At first it only seemed to make the darkness more confusing. Then I said in a low voice:

"Look! There is a man lying on the ground!"

The match went out, but in that moment I had recognised who the third prisoner was. It was my recent guest, and the cause of all my troubles, Manuel Carrera.

In the light of another match, we saw that Manuel's wrists and ankles were bound with strong cord and he was thrown like a sack of potatoes against the wall. While Juan held the light, I got at the cords with my penknife. It did not take long to saw through them. Even while I worked, I wondered why I bothered about Manuel. I knew that he did not hold my life worth a rusty nail, but I could not see him tied up, for all that. I believe I would have set him free even if I had known that his first action would be to strike me down. Or perhaps Juan's presence gave me confidence.

Manuel was not unconscious though he had been so silent. I supposed that he had been too frightened to speak. We found a chair, and sat him in it, and told him that he would be safe with us. He looked at Juan with great uneasiness, until I explained that he was in the same predicament as ourselves. Presently he recovered enough to thank us for having released him.

"And my poor Pat Hernon, you were captured after all," he said.

"I was," said I grimly. "I deserved it, too, for riding along an open road alone."

"Have you told them where the *San Sebastian* is?" he asked softly.

"That's a hard question," said I. "I have not said that I know where it is."

"Ah, so you are still playing that game," he said indulgently. "Then I will say instead: Have they asked you where the *San Sebastian* is hidden?"

"No," I said shortly. "I don't always answer questions."

But then Manuel started off on a long hysterical

argument, urging me to do what I was told and to give away all my information as soon as I was asked. I did not bother to reply after the first minute or two. He went on for a long time, clutching me and shaking me and telling me what he thought would become of me – mostly very nasty things. It was clear that he was terrified for his own skin. As he talked on, it occurred to me that he might have been promised his freedom if he could induce me to tell what I knew. At last I said to Juan:

"I don't think we should wait any longer. Manuel will betray us if we do."

Juan had been standing at the window all this time working at the catch with his knife. He got it open at this moment, and now he unhooked one of the shutters and swung it a little outwards. In the sunlight that streamed in, I saw him throw Manuel a contemptuous glance.

"He is weak," he said. "He is no good."

He closed the shutter again and came over to whisper to me:

"It is not so hard to open the window. I will go out now and see if I can pick up some information."

"But the window is at the front of the house," I protested. "Someone will see you."

"No. This is a desolate place. The men will be in the other room, talking. I will listen at the window."

"What will I do with Manuel if he has hysterics while you are gone? If he makes a noise, someone may come in and find out that you are gone."

"Manuel will make no trouble," said Juan. He went across to Manuel and stood looking down at him. "Do not speak at all until I come back," he said softly.

I remember that I congratulated myself for having got him to quell Manuel, and that I had not then the smallest knowledge of how I was being gulled.

Manuel remained silent. Juan went across to the window and slipped outside.

In the few minutes that followed, I was very much tempted to get out of that window too, and make my own escape. I knew that I did not really care what became of the two Spaniards. Juan seemed well able to look after himself – I had observed that much, at least. As for Manuel, even if I could do something to save him this time, it was likely enough that he would get himself into trouble of some other sort quite soon again. I went over to the window. One little push would open it. I would slip around the big gable rock near me and get down to the shore. Later I would pick up the road back to the town. There were other boats at the quay, among them the Spanish trawler called *San Fernando,* flying the red and yellow Spanish flag. With luck, it would be going back to Ireland. Then with my hand on the window I paused.

Supposing the trawlermen refused to take me? What if they were friends of Erik and simply handed me back to him as if I had been a stray lamb? Even if the trawlermen had never heard of Erik, they would be suspicious of me. I knew I would not be able to put up a plausible tale. But Juan would. Juan had great charm. One had only to look at him to trust him. And he was a Spaniard himself and would understand his own people. Yes, they would trust Juan as I trusted him myself. I knew that Juan would need no persuasion to come back to Ireland, if he got one hint that the *San Sebastian* was there.

I came away from the window and sat down in one of the shadowy corners. Manuel let out a long sigh, and I realised that he had been watching me closely all the time. I could not make out which side he was on, and I wondered if he would have tried to stop me if I had decided to go.

Juan had not been gone for more than a few minutes when the shutter swung suddenly open and he was in the room again. I started up. Manuel did not move. Juan said:

"They are all in the other front room, as I knew they would be. I heard a little of their talk. They will be coming here soon to question you, Pat. They are in an ugly mood."

"So am I," said I fiercely, more fiercely than I felt. "Let them question to their hearts' content – they will get no good of me."

Then Juan started in at me, trying to persuade me that it would be more prudent to tell my captors what they wanted to know. He said that my life was not worth a snap of the fingers to them.

"They seem to know all about you, Pat," he said.

135

"And they are quite certain that you have hidden the brig."

"Why should they spare my life if I tell them where it is?" said I.

And I pointed out that we were wasting time now, which should be spent in making our escape.

"A fine lot of pirates they are," said I contemptuously, "that leave three prisoners locked in a room and forget to guard the window!"

"They did not forget the window," said Juan softly. "I put their guard to sleep with a punch on the head!"

"Then we'd best be going before he wakes up," I said.

"Well, Manuel, old soldier!" said Juan. "Are you coming with us, or would you like to stay with Erik?"

"I will come with you," said Manuel.

Juan said no more, but swung the window open and stepped over the sill. I followed, and lastly came Manuel. One by one we slipped around by the big gable rock. Before I flashed out of sight of the front of the house, I had time to notice that the body of the guard was not lying where Juan had knocked him senseless. If he had crawled away to complain of his sore head to his friends, we could expect to be hotly pursued at any moment.

Down on the shore among the enormous rocks we paused. I told the other two of my plan to get aboard the *San Fernando* and persuade the trawlermen to set us ashore at Galway. Juan said that he thought this a very good idea. Manuel was silent, and I took it that he agreed too, though I would not have changed my mind for him.

The tide had gone out since the morning, and the big rocks hid our view of the sea. We climbed on to the road again, a short distance from the house, and set out to walk to the town. I looked behind at every step, prepared to fling myself over the fence into the fields at the first sign of pursuit. But we saw no one except a few men working in the fields, and these did not even raise their heads to watch us pass. With every step I felt more and more inclined to break into a run. The two Spaniards seemed quite unconcerned, and I reflected that they were probably more accustomed to this kind of excitement that I was. Manuel plodded along with his head down, like a bullock going to the fair. As for Juan, I could have sworn that he was on the point of starting up a song more that once.

At last we sighted the roofs of the town, scattered on their little hills around the horseshoe bay. The last quarter of an hour was agony. I longed to be safely on board the trawler that was to take us home, and every moment I feared that we would arrive to find the *San Fernando* steaming out of sight. I calmed down when I caught sight, between two houses, of a Spanish flag floating from a ship's mast – two narrow red stripes and a broad yellow stripe in between. I wondered why it hung a little sideways.

We skirted the town first, and then came through twisting back streets towards the quays. We passed pastry shops with delicious-looking cakes spread out in the windows, and no less tempting windows containing sausages and cooked meats and cheeses, so that I thought I would have to close my eyes to make my legs walk past them. Neither Manuel nor Juan seemed interested, and I thought in amazement that they must surely have been built without stomachs. I was glad when we left the shops behind and came down on to the quay. And then I stopped dead, while my mouth hung open with amazement.

The sea was gone.

There was the whole little bay, dry and sandy as far as the eye could see. All the boats lay on their sides, the tiny rowing-boats, so small that a man could not lie at full stretch in them, as well as the big, heavy wooden fishing boats. The *Santa Teresa* was there, and the *San Fernando* whose flag I had seen hanging sideways from its mast, lay against the quay wall for support, its keel, covered with shells and weed, resting on the shingle.

I could have burst into tears of rage. Now I remembered the men at home talking of this strange thing, which was quite unknown to us in Ireland. This was the famous low tide of Brittany.

9

The Whalers' Island

Juan turned to me with a rueful grin.

"Well, it looks as if we will have to wait for the tide," he said.

"We could carry one of the small boats down to the water – I said, hardly knowing what I said.

"And what then?" said Juan. "Would you row home to Ireland in a small boat not six feet long? No. We must wait for the tide."

"But Erik may come along at any moment," I said.

I wondered why Manuel was not having hysterics and drawing a crowd around us. Where he should have been babbling with fright, he seemed quite calm. His changes of mood amazed me.

"I have been in this place before," said Juan. "I think I know a place where we can spend the day."

"But that will be no use," I protested. "If the tide comes and the trawler sails away without us, we will be as badly off as ever."

"My friend will arrange about the trawler too," said

Juan soothingly. "He can do that without being noticed. But if we spend the day here on the quay, we are bound to attract attention."

I could see the sense of this. Juan's friend could wait until the tide was full, and then ramble along to the quays as if he were only out for a stroll. Then he could slip aboard the trawler and confer with the captain in his cabin, and later we could go aboard quietly when the little ship would be on the point of sailing. Only one thing troubled me.

"How do you happen to have been here before, and to have a friend so convenient?" I asked.

Juan shrugged.

"I have been to many places in the world, and I have many friends."

I could believe this. He was so clever, and so charming a companion that I could understand that people would take pleasure in serving him. I mumbled an apology for doubting him. He grinned at me out of the corners of his eyes.

"You are right to be suspicious. The world is full of wickedness."

I gave him an answering shamefaced grin. Then I felt Manuel pulling at my sleeve.

"People will notice us. Let us not stand here."

"Juan leads the way," I said, and from that moment I followed him blindly.

He led us through a narrow street off the quayside and up a winding, cobbled way between the houses. When I looked down I could see the roofs of the houses like steps on either side. Here, as in the fields, the people seemed too busy to do more than glance at us. This was the greatest difference between these and my own people at home, where everyone would have turned to stare, and leading questions would have been asked, and all work would have been held up while they speculated on our business and our appearance, and summoned all the neighbours to make sure that no one would miss the show. It was even more extraordinary than the difference in clothes, though that was very striking too. Here the women wore starched white net or lace caps with streamers, and the men wore light cotton suits. At home, even in the hottest summer, the women kept to their heavy red flannel petticoats and woollen head-shawls, and the men wore bawneen or bréidín, as if there was snow on the ground.

We climbed to the top of the cobbled street. The road ran along the hilltop so that we could look down at the little bay with its boats like toys high and dry on the sand. A long wall skirted the road, and when we had gone a short distance, Juan opened a green wooden door in the wall and signalled to us to go through.

We were in a neat garden laid out with apple trees and flowers, huge sunny flowers of a kind I had never seen before. At the back of the garden there was a house, granite-built and slate-roofed, with white wooden shutters. Its white door stood open on a cool tiled hall.

"Wait here," said Juan. "I will see if my friend is at home."

I watched him walk up the garden among the apple trees, and disappear through the front door, without knocking. Then I sat down on the cool grass in the shade of one of the trees. I was so hungry now that I would almost have taken a bite out of Manuel, if he had not looked a bit stringy. Whatever Juan achieved in this house, I hoped it would include a meal. The worst feature of the whole adventure was the apparent unconcern about food of my various companions. Manuel made no attempt to speak to me. It was almost as if he had forgotten the day he had spent in my house, and the story he had told me about the *San Sebastian.*

Juan was not long away. It was no more than ten minutes later that he appeared in the doorway again and beckoned to us. I got up wearily and followed Manuel, who was already on his way up to the house. When we reached the door Juan said:

"It is all fixed, as I said. My friend, Mr Janvier, will arrange everything for us. He knows the Captain of the *San Fernando,* as it happens. They sail on the evening tide, and in two days we will be in Ireland."

The thought of returning home brought tears to my eyes. I knew that Bartley must be frantic with anxiety, and blaming himself for my disappearance. I wondered if he had guessed that I had been carried off on a Spanish trawler. If his letter to Mr Daly had been found in Galway, he must know that I had passed through the town. He would know too that I had not ridden there, because the pony would have arrived home without me so soon. Bartley had probably gone to Mr Daly himself by now, and they would both be busy combing the countryside for me. I wished I could send him a quick message of some kind, to say that I was coming, but I knew that even if this could be done, it would not be safe. I began to savour in advance the welcome I would get from Mrs Folan when I would walk in her kitchen door.

Above all I wondered if Bartley had yet discovered the secret of the *San Sebastian*. When I was captured first, I had thought that I would soon know why so many people were after her. But now, after three days, I had heard nothing except Juan's claim that he owned the brig. Erik and Manuel and the others seemed determined not to mention her at all. I could not make out why they had brought me so far, unless the leader of the group had been among those whom Juan had overheard planning to question me. Now I remembered the evil faces that had waited for me behind the rock on the Galway road, and despaired of ever outwitting the person who had been so well able to plan my capture.

Manuel and I followed Juan into the house, and he shut the door after us. I was pleased at this, for I did not fancy being surprised by Erik. Juan seemed too confident for the future. I would not have been surprised to find that our enemies had tracked us here and were even now hammering at the garden gate. Juan seemed calmly certain that we had shaken them off, and that we were already as safe as if we were on the trawler bound for home.

At the end of the hallway there was a big tiled kitchen with a window looking out on a vegetable garden at the back of the house. Although it was such a warm day there was a blazing hot fire in the big stove, and the faces of the people who turned to look at us as we came in were red and shiny with the heat. The hot air that met me at the door was like to make me faint, and I staggered against Juan. He pulled out a chair and made me sit down. A fat old waddling woman in a long black skirt and a starched cap came over and peered into my face. Then she turned and cackled in a strange language to the others, waving her hands and pointing to me. She looked a kindly enough soul, and I guessed that she was offering to feed me. In any language, the tone of her voice was unmistakably that of a woman who sees a hungry boy and blames everyone for allowing him to get into such a state.

It seemed that I was right, for now she opened a press and took out the strangest loaf of bread I had ever seen. It was a good three feet long, and as thin as a walking-stick. She handed it to me without a word. I gripped it by the middle, feeling rather foolish. Then she placed a little bowl of jam on the table beside me, and showed me how to break off pieces of the bread and dip them in the jam before eating them. You may be sure I learned quickly, and

144

she heaved a long sigh of satisfaction, with her hands on her hips, as she watched me.

While I ate, I could see Juan conferring on the opposite side of the room, with a thin white-haired man whom I supposed to be Mr Janvier. I wondered if the fat woman were his wife. If she was they made a strange pair, for she was so friendly and cheerful and he so dour and cold. His eyes were like three-cornered chips of steel in his yellow-white face. When he saw that I was watching him he drew back his lips in what was meant to be a friendly smile. But I could see that he was not used to smiling, for the effort seemed to hurt him. My heart sank. I had to admit to myself that the sight of Juan's obliging friend sent me into the lowest depths of despair.

I looked across at the other occupants of the room. The first of them gave me no comfort, for he was like a younger version of Mr Janvier. He had the same hard, cold, triangular eyes, and the same long-jawed, thin, mean face, so that I thought he must be the older man's son. He was trying to look friendly too, and succeeding a little better than his father. The last person in the room was a dark-haired, dark-skinned boy of my own age. He sat on a high stool by the window and stared at me solemnly. He was the only member of the party who had not made a show of welcoming me. He sat and gazed at me unblinkingly, and I could read nothing in his face. While I worked my way down the length of the loaf, I found myself turning to look at the boy every moment. I wished he would not stare so. I was uneasy enough with that. The steady gaze he kept on me made me want to rush out of the room, and I had to remind myself that I did not have to like these people, so long as they helped me. They were a different race from mine, and it must be that I did not understand them.

When my hunger was satisfied, I laid the small remaining tail of the loaf on the table. Juan came across the room and stood smiling down at me.

"You should sleep for a few hours, Pat," he said. "We cannot go until the evening, and who knows when you will find a good bed again?"

The thought of sleep made me yawn. I was surprised at Juan for thinking of such a human need. A moment later he said:

"I think I will not sleep. I will stay here and talk to Mr Janvier, whom I have not seen for a long time."

He grinned at both of the Janviers, and the elder one smiled like a sick eel. I wondered what they could have in common. Juan spoke to the dark-haired boy:

"Show Pat a place where he can sleep."

The boy nodded and went to the door without a word. I got up and followed him out of the room, while Juan called after me heartily:

"I will call you in good time!"

Though he looked back once or twice to see that I was following him, the boy did not speak. He went up the bare wooden stairs and turned into a room at the top. It was a large room with little furniture except a wide, low bed. It was stiflingly hot. Its window looked out into the vegetable garden, so that I guessed that I was over the kitchen. I went across and opened the window, and leaned out across the sill to breathe in the sweet, fresh air.

Then I went rigid with horror. From below me a voice floated up clearly, Juan's voice, coolly tolerant as usual:

"Pat is all right," he was saying. "He thinks I am his friend. He thinks I am saving him from Erik. I am afraid he will be disappointed when we get back to Ireland, poor boy."

And he laughed, the lazy, easy laugh that had endeared him to me and had made me trust him.

Mr Janvier's hard, slightly husky voice answered him in a strange language, and I heard Juan laugh again. I turned away from the window with a coldness in my inwards. I found myself looking straight into the dark eyes of the boy who had brought me upstairs.

Panic gave me a false bravery, and in a flash I decided to make a run for it. But first I must somehow dispose of this young spy, who had probably heard the talk below as clearly as I had, and who would be quick to tell the others that I now knew that they were my enemies.

He had shut the door and was standing with his back to it. If I could get him unsuspecting, it would be easier for me. I did not want a scuffle to bring the others upstairs. With a firm eye on him, I began to move slowly across the room.

And then I had my second shock. He spoke in a whisper, so that I could hardly believe at first that I had heard him at all. I looked at him incredulously, so that he repeated his quiet remark, while amusement showed for the first time in his quiet brown eyes. For he spoke my own language, Irish, that Bartley and Mrs Folan and I, and all our neighbours in Farran and all over Connemara used daily, and that as far as I knew no Spanish boy could possibly have learned so well.

What he had said was:

"Shut the window, Pat."

When I had come to my senses again, I obeyed him, moving silently across the floor and pulling the window shut without a sound. Then I went over to where he still stood by the door and said in Irish:

"Who are you?"

"My name is Brian Mahon," he said, "and I come from Kerry, where they have men twice as good as the Connemara men."

He laughed softly when he saw the indignation in my face. I said hurriedly:

"We'll have an argument about that some other time. How did you get here?"

"I came on a Spanish trawler, called the *San Fernando*," he said. "Perhaps you saw it below at the quay. My father and mother are dead long years ago, and I didn't like the uncle I lived with, so one day the *San Fernando* came into Dingle when I was there, and I went to work on it. That is a year ago and more, and I've seen some mighty queer things in that time, and not much trawling either."

"Which side are you on?"

"If I could get away home to Ireland," said Brian, "I would not care if all the Spaniards in the world went to the bottom of the sea!"

There was such sincerity in his voice that I had to believe him. Still I hesitated before asking my next question:

"Have you ever heard of the *San Sebastian*?"

"You may be sure I have, said Brian. "They are all after her. They had her for a while, but they seem to have lost her again. They have been away searching for her, and they are setting off again this evening on the same business."

"But I thought – "

I stopped.

"Yes," said Brian. "You were meant to think that they were depending on you to tell them where the brig is. But they really mean to use you in a different way."

Suddenly I asked a question.

"Who is Juan?"

"He is the leader," said Brian.

I went over to the bed and sat down slowly. What a fool I had been! How easily I had been gulled! I had had plenty of ways of knowing that he was in league with the others. It was he who had said that the men were going to question me, and that he had knocked the guard senseless. It was he who had advised me not to make a noise on the quay when we landed. He had said that the stew was not poisoned. He had ordered Erik to put up his knife. And even at last, when I had suspected him before we came to this very house, one word from him had been enough to quiet my fears. No wonder Manuel had not been frightened!

"I deserve whatever becomes of me," I said bitterly. "I had plenty of ways of knowing that he was in league with the others."

"You need not blame yourself," said Brian. "A great many people have been deceived by Juan."

I had been very near to telling Juan exactly where to find the brig. Indeed I would have told him but for the fact that he had seemed too tame a person to be honoured with the knowledge. This was a sour recollection now.

"What do they want the *San Sebastian* for?" I asked now. "Why is she so valuable?"

"Because there are sacks and sacks full of gold on her," said Brian.

"They are not on her now," said I.

"They must be on her," said Brian. "There is enough gold on that brig to keep all the men in comfort for the rest of their lives. I've heard them talking about it over and over again."

"We found one gold piece."

Brian wrinkled his forehead in a frown.

"I can't understand that," he said. "Juan is risking a lifetime in gaol, at the very least, for that gold."

"Perhaps it was taken off the ship," I said. "Perhaps one of them deceived the others."

I was thinking of Manuel, of course, though I remembered that he too had been eager to find the brig.

"We must not talk any more now," said Brian. They might hear us. Above all they must not see that you no longer trust them."

"When next I see Juan, he'll feel the weight of my fist," I said fiercely.

"No, no!" said Brian. "Do you want to go home?"

"Of course I do."

"Then you must do as I say. Pretend to be as friendly as ever with Juan. Thank him for helping you. Let him think you are easily fooled. That way he will not watch you so closely."

"And what about you?"

"They trust me completely," said Brian. "They have even promised me a share of the loot. They have got quite fond of me, as if I were a pet dog. For a long time I have been looking for a chance of having them caught at their villainy, but they do not know that. They must not hear me speak to you, or it will be all up with me. Now get into bed and go to sleep – "

"Sleep! How can I sleep now?"

You must pretend to, then. I am supposed to sit at the door to see that you do not escape. I will be on the trawler when we sail."

151

"Will they really sail to Ireland?"

"Yes, but not straight to Galway, as Juan said. When we get to Ireland we will find a way to escape."

He slipped out of the room, closing the door quietly. Now that he was gone, I remembered many questions to which I was burning to know the answers. Where had the *San Sebastian* come from? Why was she so new and clean? Where did the history of Chile come in, and were these pirates really the descendants of Chilean Generals, as they said they were? I remembered that Manuel had said that the ship had been kept as a show-piece, and I wanted to know if this were true.

All these questions were so confusing that they made my head ache. I opened the window again and leaned out. There was a low buzz of voices downstairs now. I could not distinguish the words, but presently I heard Juan's caressing laugh. My blood boiled with rage at the thought of his treachery. I wondered how I was going to succeed in making him believe that I still trusted him. Above all, I longed to be out of this hot prison and on my way home. My only comfort was in having Brian for an ally, for without him my chances of outwitting Juan would have been miserably poor.

So the long afternoon wore on. I lay on the bed and pretended to sleep, as Brian had instructed me. But with my brain churning away as it was, by the time I heard the chairs scrape back on the stone floor below me, I was as weary as if I had run through all my travels again in the last few hours.

Presently I heard Juan's steps on he stairs. I lay back and closed my eyes. I heard him open the door softly and come towards me. Then he called me, in his gentle voice, saying that it was time for us to be on our way.

"Snake!" thought I, and looked up at him with what I hoped was a trusting smile. "Treacherous snake!"

He smiled back at me through half-closed eyes, and now that I knew him for what he was, I could see the little triumphant light in them. I started up and said that I was quite ready to go.

"Mr Janvier is on his way down to the quay," he said. "By the time we get there, he will have arranged our passage."

Of course I knew now that it had all been arranged long ago, but I managed to say that I hoped he would succeed in persuading the Captain to take us. Then I panicked as he looked at me sharply, but he only said:

"It will be all right. Mr Janvier is a very influential man."

There was no sign of Brian. When we left the house Manuel and the younger Janvier moved in on either side of me, while Juan walked a pace or two in front on the narrow street. They were making very sure that I would not escape. We walked quickly down to the quay. The tide was full now, and the

Spanish flag floated straight and proud from the mast of the *San Fernando*. It was strange to see all the little boats pulling at their mooring ropes again, like chained dogs that had woken up after sleep. The *Santa Teresa* lay farther down against the quay wall. It seemed to be quite deserted.

I could not see the elder Janvier, but as we approached a sailor's head, in a dirty old beret, popped out from behind the wheel-house and was withdrawn again. A moment later, Mr Janvier came out of the cabin with another man in creased Captain's uniform, and beckoned to us. We climbed on board.

"Into the cabin quickly," said Juan.

He hustled me in, and the others followed. Then the Captain made a great show of asking me exactly where I wished to be landed. He said that he knew the place, and had often used my house as a landmark. I could see that he had been told to be friendly, but he spoilt it all by giving a queer little evil giggle from time to time. He was quite an old man, with the smooth face of a seasoned rogue. It took all my patience to play the part of the trusting fool they took me to be.

Presently Mr Janvier went ashore. The trawlermen lost no time in casting off, and within a quarter of an hour of our arrival we were slipping away from the quay-side and out towards the mouth of the little bay. Through the porthole of the cabin, I watched the little hilly town grow smaller and smaller. The blaze of sunlight made all the windows glow. Along the waterfront the houses were reflected in the still, high tide. I thought how strange it was that I did not know the name of this place, and I wondered if I would ever see it again.

I did not see much of Juan on the voyage home. He spent a great deal of time in the Captain's cabin, where I could hear the drone of voices hour after hour. I was allowed to roam wherever I liked, and I slept in the forecastle with the crew. They were a taciturn, black-avised lot, and they took as much notice of me as if I had been one of the seagulls that wailed incessantly after the ship.

Brian seemed to avoid me. He worked hard at carrying meals and drinks to the cabin, and washing up dishes, as well as doing a series of odd jobs that the men provided for him. He never smiled, and he never spoke. He was more like a machine than a boy. Only once, in the evening, I saw him standing at the rain looking back along the ship's wake. But when he saw me moving towards him he disappeared into the little galley behind the wheel-house and I did not follow him.

Next day, in the afternoon, we stopped while the men cast the trawl nets. Presently they were hauling in a load of quivering, silvery fish. Everyone lent a hand to fill the boxes on the deck. I wondered at first why they bothered to fish at all. Then it occurred to me that if they were stopped and questioned, a few boxes of fish would serve to give an innocent look to the expedition.

It was early morning on the second day before we sighted the Irish coast. We should have seen it long before, but we had kept far out to sea, probably to avoid other ships, I thought. The early sun made a red-gold path on the water, but the light had not yet touched the dark grey mountains ahead of us when first I saw them. No one seemed at all interested except myself. I watched the land come closer hour after hour, jagged mountains brightening the day, until they were a wonderful pale transparent blue. As we approached I could pick out glittering white-walled villages with church spires, and down on the shore the tall white finger of a light-house. A mile or two off the coast there was a hump-backed island.

From the far end of the trawler I became aware that Juan was watching me. I waited, and then I saw out of the tail of my eye that he was coming towards me. A moment later he was leaning on the rail beside me.

"It is a fine thing to see the mountains of your own country again," he said easily.

"Yes, but I never saw those mountains until today."

"That is Ireland," he said, with a quick look at me.

"But not my part of Ireland," I said. "We have no light-house like that on our coast."

"You are a clever boy," he said with a laugh. "You are right, of course. This is the coast of Mayo."

"Why are we not going to my place?" I asked.

"We will go there later," he said soothingly. "We thought it better not to go straight in there. We will land here and go on to Farran by road."

"That will take a long time," I objected.

"Don't you trust me, Pat?" he asked with a smile.

I longed to shout "No!" and then to catch him by the legs and tip him overboard. But I could imagine how the crew would gather around and pitch me in after him, so that I would not be rid of his company after all. I brought out an apologetic laugh as I said:

"I won't be easy until I'm at home. I don't like the delay."

"Leave all that to me," he said. "I'll get you home in good time."

"In your own good time," I thought as I watched him walk back to the cabin.

We slowed down as we approached the island, and kept in very close. I hoped that Brian had a plan for our escape. Once on shore there would be no time to be lost. We rounded the end of the island, and I could see a village on the mainland with a little pier sticking out into the sea. A fearsome stench hung in the air. Then I saw the cause of it. On the landward side of the island there was a little pier also, just like the one I could see on the mainland. But there was no village here, nothing but a sort of stone hut with a tarred iron roof. And tied to the quay, floating on the surface of the water, were the huge carcases of several whales. A cloud of seagulls cried over them, while they pecked at the flesh and fought each other for choice pieces. My inside heaved at the sight of them, and I closed my eyes.

When I opened them again, I saw to my horror that the trawler was making straight for the island pier. I looked around frantically for Brian. There he stood in the bows, apparently unconcerned. For one wild moment I wondered if he had been deceiving me. Then he turned and looked at me, and I saw that he was as disconcerted as I was. A warning light showed in his eyes for a moment before he turned back towards the island.

Now I could see a little group of men standing on the quay. They seemed not to mind the smell of decaying whales. I supposed that they were accustomed to it. There was another trawler there, as I could see now. There was no mistaking it – it was the *Santa Teresa,* which had brought me to Brittany. It had raced us here, it seemed. As we slipped alongside I looked up at the group on the pier. I found myself looking straight into the cold eyes of Erik.

10

News of the San Sebastian

Manuel and one of the sailors came towards me. I remembered that I was supposed to be surprised, and I let out a yell for help. Juan came running from the cabin.

"Fight them, Juan!" I shouted. "Look at Erik, there on the quay!"

"I can see him," said Juan coolly. "He works for me."

I let out a long string of abuse for my betrayal. Juan smiled gently.

"Remember, I told you that the world is full of wickedness," he said. "Now, less noise, if you please, or I will let Erik cut your throat."

Now I had to pretend to be cowed, which was very far from my mood. With a good Connemara knife in my hand, I was thinking, I could have accounted for one or two of these scoundrels, before they would have overcome me. But I remembered my promise to Brian, and I knew that we must both be crafty and bide our time. I allowed myself to be led ashore.

"Into the hut, please," said Juan. "We don't want to attract attention from the village."

The hut was built on the broad flat piece at the top of the quay. It had only one small window, and I could but dimly make out the piles of whaling gear stowed at the far end. Near the door there was a table and one or two chairs, and here Juan sat and held a kind of court. The sailors stood in a little crowd between me and the door. Erik sat importantly on Juan's right hand, and Brian stood on the other side, a little behind him. If I had ever had a chance of escape, it was gone now. Erik and Juan whispered together for a few minutes, and then Juan turned to me.

"Well, Pat, my men have found the *San Sebastian*. That was a good hiding-place."

I made no answer, for I thought he was out to trick me. He went on, as if he were talking to himself:

"A fine hiding-place, you would think made to hold a brig. And a safe hiding-place too, if any place would be safe from my men. You do not believe me? Perhaps you will when I tell you that we even know the name of it. It is called the Puffing-Holes."

I stared at him blankly, but I had suffered a cruel blow. This was no trick. I wondered how they had come on her. I knew that none of the Farran men would have betrayed us. I suppose that they had come with boats by night and searched the coast until they had found her. I could imagine their delight as they swarmed all over her, soiling her decks with their dirty sea-boots, and grinding out their cheroots on her gleaming brass rail. Juan was watching me, and I was at a loss what to say. Suddenly Manuel, who had hung back until now, elbowed his way to the front of the crowd. He leaned the palms of his brown hands on the table and stretched his neck forward until his face was within a foot of Juan's.

"Did I not tell you? Did I not say the boy had her? Only for me you would not have found her!"

Juan drew away with an expression of disgust.

"Only for you! Only for you she would be anchored off the Canary Islands by now. Only for you we would all be – " He stopped and went on contemptuously a moment later: "You are a lucky man that your soul and your body are still keeping each other company, Manuel Carrera! Perhaps we were too kind-hearted. You would not be content with your share. You had to have it all for yourself. So you stole the brig and lost her. Yes, you are a lucky man that you were able to tell us where to find her, or you would be as dead this moment as any of those whales out there on the quay."

The tone of his voice was mild enough, but by the time he had finished, Manuel was quivering with fright. So this was the truth, I thought to myself. Manuel was surely the silliest pirate that ever sailed. To steal a sixty-foot brig, from such a man as Juan, and him without a single accomplice! One of my hens at home would surely have shown more wit. It was a wonder to me that they had not killed him as soon as they captured him, and I wondered now how long they would let him live to betray them again. I noticed that Juan's good humour was restored by the sight of Manuel's terror. I ventured to ask a question.

"Where is the *San Sebastian* now?"

"She is still safe in your Puffing-Holes cave," said Juan. He shrugged. "I am in no hurry to move her from such a safe anchorage."

And he looked at me blandly as if to say that we both knew this was a lie. The men who understood English growled among themselves, and Juan looked from me to them with a delighted smile. "They do not like that. They are impatient to get her away, you see." He heaved a sigh. "Well, we must let them have their way, I suppose, or there will be blood spilt."

Suddenly I asked:

"Why haven't you taken the brig out of the cave and sailed her away to the Canary Islands?"

I had guessed that there was a reason why this could not be done, and that Juan and Manuel and the Captain and the whole lot of them were somehow depending on me to help them out.

Juan looked put out at my mention of the Canary Islands. I wished I had not let him know that I had picked up the name. He had not meant to let it slip. He said in a flash:

"We question you. You do as you are told."

"Now, no hard feelings," said the Captain, who had been silent until now. He turned to me with a big, smooth, villainous smile. "Pat will help us, of course, and then we will land him in Galway and sail away, and we will never see him again."

There was a heartfelt ring about the last part, at any rate.

Now I was puzzled to know what to do. Behind these fair words there was a threat so fearful that I fancied it sprang about the dim room like an agile little red demon, peering at me with its evil face from behind every man's eyes. All at once my courage ran out through the soles of my feet, so that my knees quivered in spite of me. I could hear my heart pounding under my shirt and when I tried to swallow I found that I nearly swallowed my tongue too. The Captain clapped me on the shoulder with a huge brown paw. If he had been a bear he would have cheered me more.

"There is no need to be frightened," he said. "If you do as we say, you will be all right."

"I am not frightened," I croaked, though I knew I had the shakes by now. "You have not told me what you want."

Their plan was a simple one. It seemed that the whole barony of Farran was up in arms to save the *San Sebastian*. My heart leaped at this news. They had surprised Juan's men on the brig, and had chased them off, yelling murder and inviting them to return

163

for a pitched battle. They were generalled by a small man in spectacles and a black suit. I could not make out who this could be. I knew no one who wore spectacles. Erik seemed to have a great respect for this man, who had been the fiercest of the lot, egging the others on to launch their currachs and pursue the *Santa Teresa* out of sight.

"When did this happen?" I asked.

I was glad to notice that my interest in the story had lessened my fear.

The fight had taken place in the early hours of the morning, they said. It could not be properly called a fight because the Farran men were so numerous that Erik had been afraid to stay. They had been glad to get away with their lives, but they were very sore at the humiliation they had suffered. I nearly laughed aloud at the picture the story made in my mind. But the laugh shrivelled up and died as Juan explained his plan.

Sure enough, it all depended on me. We were to wait till nightfall, and then set out for Farran in the *Santa Teresa*. We were to cast anchor opposite the Puffing-Holes, and have a parley with whoever was on the watch. I was to be on deck, tied with ropes. And if the Farran men would not hand over the brig, I was to be let down over the side to drown before their eyes.

"You need have no fear, Pat," said Juan kindly. "It will not take them long to make up their minds between you and the brig."

I knew that this was true, and that the *San Sebastian* would be handed over without a blow struck, in return for me.

"You think it is a good plan?" said Juan.

"Excellent," I said sardonically. "How am I to co-operate? It seems to me that I need do nothing at all."

"Oh, you must cry, and beg them to save your life," said the Captain. "We will tell you when to begin. You will not find it difficult. Now just be a good boy and give us your word that you will help, and we need waste no more time."

I looked at Brian, and thought that he nodded very slightly. His face was quite blank, almost as if he had not heard a word of the strange conversation.

"Very well," I said at last.

The bear's paw slapped my shoulder again, so that I thought the bone must crack.

"Good boy!" said Juan and the Captain together, and Juan said:

"Remember, I told you once that your life is more valuable than an old boat."

That was the oddest day of my life. As soon as my decision was given, the men shuffled out of the hut. Some of them built a fire outside and roasted potatoes, while others got out a collection of weapons of all kinds and began to prepare for the battle. They took harpoons and whaling-knives from the heap at the back of the hut, and sat in the sunlight opposite the doorway cleaning and polishing them as if for a parade. Most of them had knives of their own as well, and I saw one or two guns. I stayed indoors with Juan and the Captain, and Brian brought us a meal from the trawler's galley.

When we had finished the Captain went to the door. Like a great many sailors, he never went out of doors if he could avoid it. He looked at the sky and came back and grumbled in Spanish to Juan. I guessed what he had said, and I did not know whether to be glad or sorry. Though the sun shone, there was a coolness in the air, and black clouds were massed up to the south-west. I could see that a storm was coming up, though it might be a long way off still. I wondered if it would make the men change their plans, but after a consultation they seemed to settle down again. I supposed that they had weighed the coming storm against the advantage of reaching Farran under cover of night, and had decided to wait for the dark.

The Captain went out to the trawler and came back with a greasy pack of cards. He licked his lips greedily over them, and asked me if I knew how to play. I told him that I knew one game only, and that was the game called Twenty-five.

"I know it," he said, delighted. "And so does Juan. We had an Irishman working on the whales once, and he taught it to us all." he turned to Brian, who was clearing away the plates. "Can you play Twenty-five?"

Brian nodded, and the Captain made him put away the plates and sit down to play with us. With the cards in his hand, he gave a long sigh of pure joy, like a baby with a bottle of milk. He dealt them out himself, slowly separating the dirty cards from each other, and peering at the backs as if he wished to see through to the other side.

Neither Brian nor I had any money, so we played for small Spanish coins that Juan drew from his pocket in a careless handful. Something in the way he did it reminded me of Manuel and his money-belt. Manuel had not been invited to play, and I guessed that he was still out of favour. I found it very difficult to think about the cards, and gradually all my money found its way over to the Captain's side of the table. He was divided between delight at winning and irritation with me for playing so badly.

We played for hours, until my head ached. A little moaning wind had sprung up, flapping the door in and out and wailing around the hut. The sun still shone, but with a greenish-yellow glare now, lighting up the island and the sea with an unnatural brilliance. We could hear the wash of small waves against the pier, and the trawler rubbing restlessly against its stone side. Towards evening we had another meal, but still the Captain would not let us stop. I was surprised that Juan humoured him, for he seemed to be as bored with it as we were. Still, the Captain looked like a man with a temper, and if Juan wanted something from him, he would probably have to make this concession. Erik, who seemed to be Juan's second-in-command, had gone outside with the men.

It seemed to me that the *Santa Teresa* belonged to Juan, and that the Captain, as I called him in my mind, obliged him with reinforcements from time to time.

It must have been nine o'clock when the door suddenly slammed shut. We sat motionless for a moment in the gloom. Then Juan sprang up. He wrenched the door open, so that a leaden light came in. Outside the men were silent, staring at the sky. A scatter of rain-drops, like pebbles, fell on the iron roof. The wind snatched at the door, while Juan still held it. Then it shrieked away off over the island with a mocking whistle. Juan turned back to speak to the Captain in Spanish. The whites of their eyes gleamed dully. The Captain gathered up his cards and his winnings and stowed them carefully in his pockets before he stood up.

"It is too early, but we must go now before the storm gets worse," Juan explained to me. "We will go across to the mainland and wait until dark."

I wondered what they would do then. He had not said that the storm would prevent them from setting out for Farran after dark as they had arranged. I knew those little Spanish trawlers were tough, and that they often weathered storms in which bigger ships might have foundered. But the Connemara coast is rocky and treacherous, and many a brave man would admit to being afraid of it. For myself, I blessed the storm, for now that we were to go to the mainland, we would have at least some chance of escape. Indeed I

168

had become convinced that there was no hope whatever of escape from the island, for we were under observation all the time.

We left the hut hurriedly and ran down to the quay. The men were already on the trawlers, which were lifting high on the swell while the loose gear on their decks slid about. Juan, Brian and I boarded the *San Fernando,* while Erik and Manuel went in the *Santa Teresa.* For a moment the storm stood still, with a madman's glare. We cast off, and tossed away from the little pier. Then the wind was after us again, rocking the little ship from side to side while she crawled up and down the long, dark waves. Strands of seaweed whirled past as the floor of the ocean was churned up. High, high overhead, the wind roared its wild song. Every rope on the rigging hummed the chorus. Huddled on the shore of the island the seagulls wailed and cried, the loneliest sound in all the world. I looked back and saw the *Santa Teresa* ploughing after us, with spray dashing up to her gunwale. Sometimes she seemed to disappear under the waves, to rise again dripping like a sea-monster a moment later.

As we neared the mainland, we were sheltered a little by an arm of land, which, with the little pier made a sort of harbour. Even the experienced sailors breathed a little more freely when we had left the hurrying storm behind. The Captain walked past me where I stood on the deck and called out to Juan:

"It's going to be a dirty night!"

The wind caught the words and flung them away over the black water. I looked at Juan, who was leaning on the rail in the stern. A change had come over him. His eyes glowed with a wild light, and he balanced on his feet like a dancer against the storm. He was no longer the easy, tolerant person I had known up to now. At that moment I could see why he was the leader, and why the men followed him with such devotion. He was an extraordinarily handsome fellow, and this new vitality made him a person to be trusted with one's very life. Not with mine, of course. For me, he was now ten times more dangerous than he had been. I could guess that if I obstructed him now, I would be swept aside like a stone kicked from a path. He shouted hilariously to the Captain above the wind:

"We have been out on dirtier nights than this!"

The Captain grumbled to himself, but made no answer. I could see that he, too, had observed Juan's change of mood, and would be careful not to cross him.

A few minutes later we were sliding along by the quay while the wind howled and raged on the other side of the high wall. The swell lifted us up and down, and the water was heavy and opaque, but we were safe enough for the time being. It was not yet quite dark. I could see the outlines of houses a short distance away on a road that ran up from the quay. There were low thatched roofs and higher slated ones. Away up behind them there was a high green

170

mountain, with bare rock at the top. A sheltered village, unless the wind was from the sea.

I thought we would sit on the trawlers until the wind would fall, or until it darkened some more. But to my surprise Juan and the Captain stepped ashore almost at once. On the quay they hesitated and turned back. Juan called out:

"You must come along too, Pat! you are too valuable to be trusted to anyone but myself."

Silently I stepped ashore. Out of the tail of my eye I saw Brian come from behind the deck house. He called out boldly:

"May I come too, please?"

"Quickly, then!" said Juan, and turned impatiently towards the village.

Brian sprang ashore like a cat, and had reached us in a second. We marched briskly up the quay. It had grown much darker in the last few minutes. The sky was full of scrappy indigo clouds. I could see that night would fall early, on account of the storm. It would be a black night too, for the moon was clouded over. In that blackness lay our chance of escape.

When we reached the village, lights were streaming from the cottage windows. The doors were all shut against the gale. We stopped before a public-house with a sign hanging above, and Juan had to hammer several times on the door before he was heard above the noise of the wind. At last the door opened enough to allow us all to slip through. The sudden shaft of light lit up the sign. I read the name, "The Golden Cockerel", under the feet of a stout and arrogant gold bird with upraised beak and stiff fanned tail. The door shut behind us, sending a blue cloud of turf-smoke up to the rafters.

We were in a big kitchen which also served as a bar. Bottles and barrels were ranged in one corner. A large turf fire burned on the hearth, and a number of men sat on stools and chairs at either side of it. They had all turned towards the door as we came in, and when the smoke cleared away I saw that each man held a glass of black porter in his hand, slightly lifted, as if they had all been about to drink, but had stopped to stare at us. Another man, probably the owner of the public-house, stood with his back to the door where he had remained after having let us in. From their clothes I guessed that they were the men of the village, gathered in here on a stormy night because they could not go fishing.

When Juan spoke it was almost as if a spell had been broken. All the men let out a sigh, and then hastily lifted their glasses and drank. With a foreign accent which I knew he did not usually have, Juan had said:

"Can we have a little drink while we wait for the storm to blow off?"

"That will be a while, I'm thinking," said the publican.

He drew a glass of brandy for each of the men and cocked an eye at us.

"Lemonade for the young lads?" he said.

Juan nodded. The Captain grumbled to himself, but stopped when he saw that Juan was going to pay. Then he smiled and nodded to us the told us to drink up like good boys.

Neither Brian nor I spoke a word. We sat, holding our glasses, on a bench by the wall, well back from the fire and out of the little pool of light cast by the single oil-lamp. This bench ran the whole length of the wall and finished at the back door. Brian had chosen it, and I soon understood why. As the men began to talk to Juan and the Captain, he edged closer and closer to the back door. No one noticed. I moved along too, and then we waited before we ventured it again.

For a while the men talked about the weather, and the likelihood of boats along the shore being damaged. Most sensible people would have their boats ashore, they said, so that they would be out of harm's way. But a man might be away from home, selling a cow, perhaps, or buying a few sheep, and he would come back to find his boat smashed up. That would be a terrible thing, they said, unless he had good neighbours. I thought of the *San Sebastian,* and wondered if she were getting uneasy in her cave. I thought she would be safe enough for the present, unless the wind shifted more to the south. If this happened, long waves would race through the cave, breaking with a crash and a shaft of flying spray against the rocks at the back. The *San Sebastian* was

173

moored to those rocks. I wondered how long the mooring-ropes would hold. In my mind's eye I could see her being drawn out of the cave on the long backwash, and sailing off high and free under her tall masts. Then I saw her battering helplessly on the black rocks until she foundered and sank. Tears pricked my eyelids at the vision of it.

Brian moved along the bench again and brought me to my senses. I looked across the room and saw the Captain and Juan looking very uneasy. Their glasses had been refilled. Juan's eyes were shifting quickly from side to side. Drops of sweat stood out on the Captain's temples. For a moment I was puzzled and then I saw that the village men were all leaning forward eagerly, mouths half open, a gentle, appreciative smile on every face. I knew that expression well. I could see at once that they were at the favourite Connemara game of expertly questioning unwilling strangers. They were taking the questions in turn, one to each man.

"Would you be foreign sailormen?"

"Would you be from Spain?"

"What class of a boat have you?"

"What is the fishing like?"

"What is the fishing like on a stormy night?"

"Why didn't ye go into Kilronan with all the other Spaniards? Kilronan in the Aran Islands – don't ye even know where it is?"

"What brings ye this way?"

The short answers of Juan and the Captain

convinced the men that they had two dark horses in the house. This was what they always hoped for. They prodded and poked with their questions until Juan could stand it no longer. Suddenly he stood up and tossed off the remains of his drink. His chair fell back with a crash on the stone floor, but he did not pick it up. He clapped the Captain on the shoulder and said heartily:

"Time for us to be off! Come along, boys!"

By this time we had reached the end of the bench. It was pitch dark now, as I could see from the crossed black square that was the uncurtained window. A row of backs separated us from the two Spaniards. When Juan spoke the men turned their heads to look at us. They had clearly forgotten all about us. They peered into the gloom of the alcove where we were. Brian waited for no more. He snatched at the latch and flung the back door open. He grasped my wrist and we plunged outside. Just before I slammed the door shut behind us, I saw how Juan had leaped after us, but had been held in check by the men. I knew they would see their chance of revenge now, for the unanswered questions. I prayed that they would delay our pursuit by even a few minutes. Then I was scrambling up the grassy hill with Brian.

11

We Start for Home

A hundred yards up the hill we flung ourselves down and panted for breath. We had climbed several stone walls and had crossed a briar patch and a furze thicket, so that our shins and feet were bleeding from various wounds. I felt the blood trickle warmly over my bare toes.

"Are you all right, Pat?" Brian whispered urgently.

"Only scratches," I answered. "And you?"

"The same."

Shoulder to shoulder on the grass, we looked down the hill towards the village. A hubbub of excited voices and the sound of feet running were carried up to us on the wind. The back door of the "Golden Cockerel" was open again, and dark figures crossed in front of it while we watched.

"I think they are looking for us in the street," said Brian. "They have not yet thought of the hill."

"They'll get no help from the village people," said

I. "Perhaps they'll even be able to send them off in the wrong direction."

We were still uncomfortably close to our pursuers, and we waited only to get our breath before moving on again. As we climbed, the wind became stronger, and presently we had to go on all fours to keep ourselves from being rolled down the slope. Now we had to follow the shoulder of the hill, for it had become too steep for climbing. Suddenly I realised that we were on a path, a sort of sheep-track no more than a foot wide. I grasped Brian's sleeve and whispered:

"This will lead us down to the village!"

We stopped uncertainly, fighting against panic. Brian's voice was hoarse as he said:

"We could go along this track for a piece – "

His voice trailed off, and I felt his arm shake in my hand. I listened for a second before I heard it – feet running along the path towards us. Horror stricken, I pushed Brian before me up the steep slope beside the path. A stone rolled under my foot, but the thundering hooves of the wind drowned its rattle. Then Brian fell. And at that moment I felt a large hand on my shoulder. I gave myself up for lost.

My terror was so great that it was some little time before I understood the words that were murmured into my ear. It was a soft, gentle voice, speaking in Gaelic. Tears of relief sprang into my eyes. I forced myself to listen.

"Get up," said the voice. "Hurry!"

I stumbled to my feet. Between us, the stranger and I lifted Brian, still dazed from his fall, and half walked, half carried him between us. Those last ten yards to safety were like a horrible dream. On the path I could hear our pursuers plunging about searching for us, and it seemed that at any moment they must look up and see us outlined against the sky. And whatever was to become of us, I knew that I could not run another step.

"Quick! Get inside!" the voice instructed us. "Stoop down!"

I did so, and found myself being pushed into a hole, like a doorway, in the mountain-side. I dragged Brian with me. I did not need the warning to keep still, for I was quite unable to move, and I had no breath left for talk.

We were in a sort of bothy, cut out of the hillside, lying on the earthen floor. It was pitch dark, with not even a greyness about the doorway. I wondered if a sheep skin hung there, to keep out the cold. I had not felt it brush my face as we had pushed our way in.

A weird shout came from below, borne on the wind. A voice from the doorway answered.

"What's the matter with you, mister?"

"Did you see two boys go past here?" came Juan's voice.

The voice of our rescuer answered with a laugh:

"Two boys on the mountain, is it, on a night like this?"

Juan's voice was closer, as he said impatiently:

"Yes, yes. Two boys. Did you see them?"

"How could I see them, and it pitch dark? There isn't a sheep, same, out on the mountain tonight."

"What are you doing here, then?" asked Juan suspiciously.

"Watching out for the lobster-boats," said our friend easily. "'Tis a dirty night, and they'll be wanting help to land. I'll see their lights out at sea from up here, and I'll be down at the quay before them."

"Are you a lobster-fisher?" asked Juan.

It was clear that he was puzzled to find a man sitting on the mountainside during a storm, and he did not know whether to believe him or not.

"That's right, mister. I didn't like the look of the weather tonight, so I stayed behind, but the others were all for going, so I said to them, 'Let ye be going, so, and I'll go up on the mountain and watch out for ye coming back, if ye ever come back – '"

"Yes, yes," said Juan impatiently.

I heard him stamping off, and the lobster-fisher's mocking voice calling after him:

"Goodbye, mister, and good luck!"

Now I could hear the wind sweeping up the hill with a swift wild whistle. It was queerly still in the bothy, for there were no windows and doors to rattle, and the roof was the heavy turf of the hill.

Suddenly I found that I could see the grey patch of the doorway through which we had come. Then as I watched it darkened again, and the voice of our friend said:

"The rain is starting at last. I'm coming in."

Then I realised that he had been sitting with his back in the doorway, filling it completely. Juan standing outside need not have known of the bothy's existence. I reached out a hand and found Brian in the darkness. I felt his hand grip mine. We had not spoken a word since we had first heard Juan's running feet on the path.

"Are ye there at all?" said the impatient voice of our friend. "I never before heard two boys with less talk. Tell me now, have ye a tongue between ye, even?"

A match cracked, held aloft in a huge hand, and we stared at each other in its light. I saw an immense man, fully six feet and six inches in height, and as broad as my kitchen door, sitting on the earthen floor with his knees drawn up like a monkey. He was dressed in homespuns, like my own people, and he wore a pair of rawhide shoes such as the Aran Islanders wear. He swung his heavy head from one to the other of us, examining us with wondering eyes. At last he said, as the match went out:

"Glory be to Heaven! Where did ye two garlachs come from?"

"We came on a trawler with the Spaniards," I said.

"Was that one of them that passed by?"

"Yes."

He paused to consider.

"You'll not be very friendly with him, I'm thinking?" he said delicately.

The understatement made me laugh aloud. The big man said:

"Ah. That's what I thought."

There was another pause. I could hear the rain now, falling with a steady drumming sound outside. Somewhere in the corner of the bothy there was a trickle of water that started and stopped and started again. After a moment he struck a second match, and lit a candle-end which he took from one of his pockets. In the dim light I could see that the ceiling of the bothy was lined with interlaced wattles. There were several bundles of dried ferns on the floor, and these and a big old iron cooking-pot were the only furniture of the place.

"They call me Martin Mór," the lobster-fisher went on. "Now tell me who you are, so that we can be more friendly."

I told him my name, and that I lived in Farran. He had been there once, he said, and he remembered several of the men that he had met in Matt Faherty's shop. Then he made Brian tell him his name and place too. All this time he never stirred, for he was again blocking the doorway with his broad back, so that I was sure no gleam of light could escape. Suddenly he asked:

"Are ye hungry? Would ye like some porridge?"

We were ravenous, for we had not eaten since we had left the island. The lemonade at the "Golden

Cockerel" was long forgotten. The mention of food almost brought tears into my eyes, and I could only nod my answer.

"Fetch over that pot," said Martin. "I can't stir from here as long as we have the light."

I brought the heavy pot and placed it on the floor between myself and Brian. When I lifted the lid I found that it was half full of cold porridge.

"Is the spoon there?" asked Martin anxiously.

It was, a horn spoon, which must have been a great age, for it was worn thin with use.

"You'll have to take turn about," said Martin. "We have but the one spoon."

The porridge was coarse and lumpy and as cold as stone, but we ate it politely, taking turns with the spoon. Martin watched us carefully to see that we were enjoying it. When he had finished he said:

"Ah, there's nothing like a good meal of porridge to warm the inside. And if the porridge is cold same, 'tis a cold man wouldn't warm it. Ye're out of luck tonight, for we often have a sup of goat's milk to go with it."

We said it was such fine porridge that it needed no milk.

"'Tis all that," said he solemnly. "I made it myself. Tell me now, why were ye running away from the Spaniard, and why did he talk to me like a man that has a grip of his knife-handle in his pocket? Ye look two harmless enough lads."

"It's all because of a piece of wrack that Pat

found," said Brian. "They want it, and Pat has it, and they won't stop at killing to get it."

"A valuable piece of wrack," said Martin. "What would it be, now?"

"A boat," said Brian.

"An old-fashioned sailing-ship," I said. "Only for me she would have been battered to pieces on the rocks."

I told him about the arrival of Manuel, and how he had been carried off by force from my house, and about my own kidnapping as I rode the pony into Galway for help.

"And now Bartley probably thinks I'm dead," I said, "and the Spaniards are on their way to Farran to get the brig."

"They won't be on their way in this storm, I'm thinking," said Martin. "They'll have to lie below at the quay for a few hours anyway."

I started up.

"Then we can be off now and get to Farran before them – "

"Not so fast, boy. It's fifty-five miles from here to Farran by road. Ye only have a few hours. This storm won't last much longer. Listen to the wind!"

It was still blowing strongly, but the whistle had gone out of it. Martin quenched the candle between finger and thumb and moved aside from the doorway so that we could all look out. The rain still fell heavily, so that we could not see the lights of the village. I wondered if the men had gone back to the

"Golden Cockerel" to talk over the excitement of the evening. If Juan had given up the hunt for us, he would be back on the trawler by now, trying to persuade the reluctant Captain to put out into the storm.

"We can't delay any longer," I said urgently. "We must get home to Farran at once."

"That can be done," said Martin slowly. "Tell me now, are you any hand with a horse?"

"As handy as I'd be with a boat," I said eagerly. "And Brian, here, would be the same. Can you get us horses?"

"That's the trouble," said Martin. "I could get you one horse, but I couldn't get two. Two horses is a very hard thing to get."

"One horse would be better than no horse," said I. "If he's big, he'd maybe take the two of us."

"He's big, all right," said Martin. "Near as big as myself." He laughed, a low, soft chuckle. "It will give me great pleasure to get you that horse."

Something in the way he said it made me ask:

"Are we talking about your own horse?"

"He belongs to my brother."

"Will you ask your brother for him?"

"Faith and I won't! My brother wouldn't give a sup of milk to a starving cat."

"Well then, how will you get him?"

"I'll steal him, of course," said Martin heartily.

"From your own brother!" I exclaimed, shocked.

"Now, listen to me, young fellow," said Martin,

184

and I could see that he was deeply offended. "I'll give you a sound piece of advice. As long as you're roaming the country, keeping company with a pack of thieving Spanish pirates, you'd best not be criticising anyone that has shown himself a friend to you. How do I know what you've been up to? Maybe I was too ready to believe that story you told me about a sailing-ship. A mighty unlikely tale it sounded to me, I may as well tell you! But did I question it? No. I hid you from the Spaniard in my own bothy, and gave you my good porridge for your supper, and all I get for thanks is to be told that I'm a thief and a rogue. Maybe you'd like to be stepping down that path now, and finding your own way to Farran, if that's where you come from at all!"

I was deeply ashamed at having treated him so. I called myself a fool too, in as many ways as I could think of, for having thrown away such a friend. How were we to get to Farran now? All at once, I despaired of ever seeing the *San Sebastian* again. Then I heard Brian say easily:

"Pat doesn't mean any offence, Martin. I'm thinking there's a tale of some sort behind what you said, enough to make anyone curious."

I was relieved to hear Martin chuckle again. Then he said:

"Right enough, 'twas a queer thing to say, and I'll tell you why I said it." He laid his huge hand on my arm. "You'll not be cross, Pat, agrá. Sure, I didn't mean a word of it. If you had gone off down the mountain, I'd have been after you before you'd be gone five steps."

I assured him that I was not offended, and he went on:

"My brother is a small weedy little fellow. He's that crafty and mean that I'd swear he didn't ever eat enough, and that's why he's so small. You wouldn't think I'd have a brother like that, now, would you?"

We agreed solemnly that we would not.

"He has a thin, prim, bullrush of a wife that's as bad as himself for minding the ha'pence. They have a tight little farm below there," he waved his hand, "and they keep a miserable leprechaun of a servant-boy to work for them. They watch every bite the creature puts into his shivering jaws, and every time they pay him his poor wages they give him a lecture on the bad times that's in it, and tell him that they're depriving themselves of their coffin-money for him."

"They don't sound like people that would willingly lend a horse," I commented.

"True for you, Pat. Sure they even grudge the bit of manure to grow the crops. Well, there a while back, the brother came along to me with a proposal, as he called it. I was to leave the lobster-fishing, and come down and work for him, he said. I was not to get paid, but if himself and the wife died before me, I could have the farm."

"'Live, horse, and you'll get grass!'" said Brian.

"The very thing I said to him!" said Martin, delighted. "I told him he was the meanest, skinflintiest, old rasper in the country, and that I wouldn't set foot in his mangey farm the longest day I live. Before that he'd lend me the horse an odd old time, grudgingly enough. But since then I haven't seen hair nor hide of the beast. I would give me great pleasure to borrow him and lend him to two young lads like yourselves, for a good cause."

We thought this over in silence for a minute or two. If we did not injure the horse, we could send him back to his owner in a day or two, and apart from the likelihood of his being tired, there would be no harm done. Certain it was that we could not afford to be squeamish about borrowing him without leave. There was so little time to be lost.

"Very well," I said. "We'll borrow the horse, if we can, and if anything happens to him, we'll pay your brother his price."

"That I'm sure you will," said Martin, "though if you don't I'll lose no sleep. To work, now!"

We jumped up without further delay. I was glad to find that, unpalatable as it was, the cold porridge had restored my energy. Brian had got out his knife and was sharpening it on a stone by the doorway. Martin searched in the darkness until he found a coil of rope.

"This will have to do you for a bit, bridle and reins," he said, "and the seat of your breeches for a saddle."

Before we left the bothy, he carefully moved the pot, with the remains of the porridge, back against the wall. Then we went outside.

The rain had stopped in the last few minutes, leaving the mountainside running with water. Martin led us down at an angle, so that we came to level ground at the end of the village street away from the sea. Though he was so big, he moved as silently as a cloud-shadow in his rawhide shoes. Even we in our bare feet made more sound. We paused for a moment and glanced down the street. I knew it was late now, for only one or two lights showed in the windows. At the far end, a duller light rose and fell on the trawler against the quay wall. Martin gripped us each by an elbow, and we turned away from the village.

We had not far to go. We followed the broad grass strip by the road for a piece, until we came to a causeway over the ditch and a gate into a field. Martin went over and leaned his elbows on he gate, and we did the same, one on either side of him. A star or two had appeared, and a dim grey light came from the still stormy sky.

What followed was the oddest thing I had ever seen. We stood there, leaning on the gate for several minutes, while Martin talked gently in horse language. That is the only way in which to describe it. He made soft little clicking sounds with his tongue, on different notes, and once he gave a very gentle whinny. Presently we became aware of movement in the field, and then we could make out a dark patch moving towards us. It came closer, breathing heavily with little snorts. Now we could make out the shape of a tall, finely-built horse, picking its way slowly and nervously towards us. Still Martin talked on, in that strange little clicking whisper, until the horse came right up to the gate and laid its head on his shoulder. There they stood, rubbing noses and conversing quietly like two Christians. It was all I could do to keep in the wild guffaw that rose up in me.

"Come over and talk to him, Pat," said Martin out of the side of his mouth.

Brian was already stroking the horse's neck and murmuring to him. While I followed suit, Martin was quietly drawing back the bolt of the gate. A moment later he swung it open and led the horse outside. I held it by the mane while he swung the rope over its head. A few quick knots made a bridle and a reins.

"Up with you," whispered Martin. "The sooner you get out of this parish, the better."

He gave a leg up to each of us. I went in front, and Brian sat behind me with his thumbs hooked in my belt. Then Martin handed me the reins. The horse scraped the grass with a hoof, and I felt it shiver with excitement under me.

"Which road to we take?" I asked.

"Straight as the barrel of a gun from here to Cong," said Martin. "You can't miss it. Do you know the way from Cong to Farran? You go through Cornamona – "

"Where the bees go barefoot," said I. "I know it like I know my own name."

"Then you must only keep going till you get there. Keep to the grass by the side of the road as long as you can, for it's kinder to the horse's feet. Treat that horse well, for he's a friend of mine."

"How will I sent him back?" I asked suddenly. "I don't even know the name of this place."

"I'll come for him, in a few days," said Martin. "I'll be dying with curiosity till I hear the end of your story."

This suited me well, for I knew that Bartley would be glad of a chance to thank him for helping us.

We waited for no more. I leaned forward and tickled the horse's neck. He plunged into a gallop at once, so that I felt Brian clutch my belt to save himself. Martin called softly:

"Good luck to ye!"

With the breath knocked out of me, I could only wave my hand to him, though I thought he could hardly see me in the darkness. Then we were bounding off down the road, our ears full of the drumming music of hooves on turf.

12

The San Sebastian *Sails Again*

It was not long before the horse settled down to a steady trot. He seemed quite unconcerned at finding two passengers on his back instead of one. It was almost as if Martin Mor had told him the story of the *San Sebastian,* and that he was anxious to help us. Or perhaps he was simply glad to put a distance between himself and Martin's mean brother. Whatever the reason, his pace never slackened, except when I forced him to walk down the steeper hills. A stumble and a fall now would have been a cruel disappointment.

It was a desolate country, for the most part, through which we rode. A deep ditch of water on either side was all that separated the marshy fields from the road. It was well for us that a flying moon among ragged clouds gave us enough light. There was not a soul abroad. We would have fancied ourselves in the country of the dead, but for the odd lone bark of a sheepdog, or the solitary light in a farm byre away down among the fields. The horse's trotting hooves made little noise on the wet grass, so that presently we began to talk in low voices.

Since first I had laid eyes on Brian in Mr Janvier's house in Brittany, this was the first occasion on which we had found ourselves alone, with time for conversation. He told me that he came from the village of Ballyferriter, in Kerry. The land is greener there than in Connemara, he said, but it is none the less poor for that. An idea was turning itself round and round in my mind, like a dog looking for a comfortable spot for a sleep before the fire. At last I said cautiously:

"You won't be able to go back and work for Juan, after having deserted him like this."

"Go back?" He laughed. "No, I cannot do that."

"What will you do, then?" I asked carelessly.

"I don't know," said Brian slowly. "I could go back to Ballyferriter on a visit, perhaps, and find out how they have got on without me. I'd like to climb Sybil Head again, and look out for miles over the sea on a clear day. And I'd like to see Ferriter's Castle, and the cave below where Pierce Ferriter hid his wife while he fought his enemies, only the tide came in and she was drowned before he could come back. And there's a little point called Fort Doloro where there was a battle between the Spaniards and the English once, in a little fort over the sea, and they say the fields around are full of skeletons toe to head, to this day."

"Well, I must say yours is a doleful part of the world, and no mistake!" said I. "I don't know what you want going to visit all those miseries, when you could stay with me and have fun, and farm and fish and call in to Bartley's in the evening for a bit of music and story-telling around the fire."

Brian began indignantly:

"My part of the country is the most beautiful in the whole world – "

His voice trailed off, and I could feel his grip tighten on my belt with excitement. Suddenly he burst out:

"Do you mean I could live with you, in your house? And never go home at all? And not go cabin-boy on another trawler?"

"Well, you would miss the fun of that, to be sure," I said. "But you won't want for a sail in one of our pookawns." His silence made me uneasy, and I went on persuasively: "We go to the Aran Islands in the poookawns with turf, and we have other sailing-boats called nobbies, and a small kind that's meant for pleasure only, called gleoteogs. Then I have my own currach, and if we save the *San Sebastian* we'll have that too – "

I might have gone babbling on forever, if he had not interrupted me.

"That's enough! Soon you'll be telling me that you have a whaling-ship or an ocean liner. Do you think I need promises like that before I'll come with you? The only thing is – what will Bartley think?"

"Bartley will be as pleased as if I had brought home a particularly big fish," I said. "You wait and see."

So it was settled, and as we rode along through the darkness, I began to run over in my mind the places I would take Brian, the things I would show him, and the people he would meet. But above all I thought of the joy it would be to show him the *San Sebastian* at last, and to explore every inch of her in his company.

We were thankful that the rain did not start again. The sky had cleared a little too, so that the moonlight showed up a broad gleam of water ahead of us.

"That will be Lough Corrib," I said, pointing to its eerie glitter. "If it were daylight, you could see all the little islands covered with trees."

The road was high and bare here, and we were able to make out whitewashed gables peering from among the trees near the lake. Presently we saw the dark clutch of houses that was the village of Cong. I pulled up the horse as we approached it.

"Must we go through the village?" Brian whispered. "Perhaps we can keep to side roads instead."

"The lake is at one side," I said, "and I don't know the roads at the other side. It would not do to get lost."

The horse swished his tail as if in agreement, and stamped a hoof on the grass, impatient to be off again. I stroked his neck to quieten him, while we looked down at the dark landscape. Not a light showed anywhere, and one would have thought the people were all so fast asleep that we would be quite safe in trotting boldly through the village. But I knew better. In imagination, I could see first one head and then another popping out of hastily opened windows, the silence for a moment, and then the first shout:

"Who is that?"

"What's the hurry, mister?"

"At this hour of the night!"

Then conversation would start between themselves.

"Maybe it's a runaway horse."

"Johnny! Did you leave the gate of the big field open?"

"No, no! That's no runaway! I saw two boys on its back."

"Ha! Horse thieves! After them!"

"Hey, lads! Wait for us!"

Then doors would begin to open and the people would stream out, men, women and children, all eager for a night's sport. We would be lucky if we got away from them.

"We must get through the village somehow," I said.

"Perhaps we would carry the horse," said Brian sardonically.

"That would be fine," I said, and stopped suddenly, as an idea occurred to me. I slid to the ground. Quick! Get down!" I whispered to Brian. "Have you a woollen jersey?"

I was slipping off my own as I spoke. Brian took off his jacket and pulled his jersey over his head.

"Now, your knife," I said. "Cut the jersey in two!"

"Cut it in two!"

"Yes, for duffle shoes for the horse. Our only chance of getting him through the village is to keep him quiet. I learned that trick from Erik himself, on the way into Galway in the trap," I explained. "They are well versed in all the tricks. I have some string in my pocket to tie on the pieces."

I had my own knife in my hand by this time, and had set to work on my jersey. It was a wonderful white one, full of intricate patterns. Mrs Folan had knitted it for me only last winter. It was dreadful to have to destroy it, I thought, as I cut the first thread. It was extraordinarily difficult and slow work. My knife had been used for every possible purpose, from cutting up bait to whittling grips on a pair of oars, so that it was sadly blunted. My patience had run out long before I had come to the end. Brian's knife was in better condition, and his jersey several years older, so that he had begun to tie on his pair of duffle shoes before I held my two pieces ready in my hand. I went to help him, while the horse obligingly lifted on foot after another. Brian wrapped a piece of cloth around and under each hoof, and then I tied them securely with lengths of string. In a few minutes we had done.

"Now you're the height of grandeur," said Brian to the horse. "You never thought you'd live to wear a couple of pairs of socks with your shoes."

The horse shook his head.

"But don't forget they're not only for show," I reminded him. "And don't give a hearty whinny in the main street of Cong."

He turned a reproachful look on me, while the moonlight gleamed on the big shiny whites of his eyes.

"See that?" said Brian. "There is no need to insult him."

So we said a few polite things while we climbed on his back and moved off again. We tried him on the road for a little piece, and found that the ring had gone out of his iron shoes. Then we moved back on to the grass again.

The horse moved slowly and awkwardly at first until he became accustomed, I suppose, to the feel of his new stockings. Before we had reached the village, however, he had begun to trot again, contentedly enough.

My heart was thundering as we approached the first houses. Brian sat rigidly behind me, and I could almost feel him holding his breath. I made the horse walk, and he picked his way so gently that he made little more noise than a dog. After a minute or two I shook the reins, because I thought him too slow. He quickened his pace a little, and I saw his ears twitch nervously in the moon's thin light. We were almost halfway along the street when I patted his neck and urged him into a trot. Now he could not help making noise, but it was so soft and dull a sound that I hoped the sleeping people would think it was a dream. Even while I thought of this, I knew it was a vain hope.

The end of the street was in sight, and the dark country beyond, when the first window was thrown up. Sure enough, a man's voice called out:

"Who's that?"

I waited for no more. I kicked the horse's flanks with my bare heels, and shouted to him. He broke into a gallop at once. I could imagine the astonished head and shoulders of the questioner, craned out of the window to see us go. Already other windows were being flung up and questions hurled after us. But long before the people could stagger downstairs, we were out of the village, away off into the darkness again. The horse's iron shoes rang like bells again, for the duffle shoes were quite worn through. That did not matter now. They had served their purpose.

We were panting as much with excitement as with the exercise when we slowed down again. Off on our left, the long lake stretched as far as we could see, with dark patches where the islands were. We stopped to listen. The wind that had followed us all night carried no sound of pursuers.

"I think they must have gone back to bed," I said.

"I hope that first man fell out of the window," said Brian savagely. "Did you see him?"

"No. I was watching the road."

"I turned back to look," said Brian. "He was as

thin as a snake, or an eel. He had a long, thin, wandering neck and a long, flat head – "

"How could you see all that in the dark?" I asked in wonder.

"I saw it, all right," said Brian. "It would be a poor thing not to be able to see in the dark."

"A useful man on a night's fishing," thought I, and I determined to have more talk with him at some other time on this subject.

After a while the road left the lake behind, and took a high, lonely way between huge mountains. It was desolate beyond belief here, in the darkest part of the night, and we fell silent from depression. The warm feel of the horse between our knees was our only comfort, and he seemed determined not to flag for a second. At last we began to go downhill towards the sea, and I knew we were on the last stage of our journey.

"That must be the dawn," said Brian, as a line of pale green light appeared on the horizon. "How much farther is it?"

"About ten miles," I said. "It will be daylight by the time we reach Farran."

"The storm is not over yet. See those heavy black clouds. It will be a dirty day at sea."

The pale green strip of light widened, between tossing indigo sea and lowering indigo clouds. As the day brightened we could see how the white caps were blown off the big waves. When we came nearer to the coast we saw wild spray dashing on rocks and heard the thundering roar of the sea.

We covered the last few miles in complete silence. I was all amazed to find the familiar bushes and walls still in their accustomed places, and the quiet houses that we passed still standing where they had always stood. Everything looked strangely small and helpless, to such a travelled man as myself – even the Minaun mountain with its little horns grown no longer since last I had seen them. Quietly we came to the boreen down to Bartley's house, and quietly turned in on to it's rough stone paving.

At last the horse admitted that he was tired, with drooped shoulders and hanging head. Once or twice his hooves rolled a little on the loose stones, and I had to pull his head up to save him from a fall. Then we clattered into the yard at the gable of Bartley's house.

It was no more than five o'clock in the morning. We were both heavy with sleep. We slid off the horse's back stiff and weary, and hardly able to walk. We staggered around the gable and past the kitchen window to the door. I heard a shriek, that made me pause stupidly on the threshold, and then Mrs Folan was all around us, it seemed, laughing and crying at the same time, wiping her tears on her check apron, hugging me, scolding me and calling me all the abusive and endearing names she could think of. It was like being caught up in a small fat whirlwind in a red petticoat and a plaid head-shawl.

At last I began to recover myself enough to bring Brian forward, while I observed that even at that hour of the morning the kitchen was full of our neighbours.

Mrs Folan shook hands with Brian and led him over to the fire while she said:

"Indeed and you're heartily welcome, and you'll have a cup of tea now, before we do anything else."

In a matter of seconds she had cups in our hands and was standing there beaming at us.

Bartley had not sat silently through this. He had jumped up from his seat on the hob as we came in, and he danced about impatiently behind his wife waiting to get in a word. Now he stood in front of us and said:

"Where in the world did ye drop from?"

I told him my adventures in a few words, while the men sitting about the kitchen gave little cries of amazement.

"To think that all this could happen right here in Ireland!" said the tailor, shaking his head.

"Now, if it happened in America you could understand it," said little Joe Fahy. "They say terrible things are happening in America every day of the week."

The tea had wakened us up, and I began to remember more and more of the story.

"You had a visit from the whalers yourselves," I said.

"We had, so," said Bartley, and all the men grinned

201

appreciatively. "When you disappeared, we set a guard on the brig day and night. Not exactly on her, you understand, but up on the cliff-top with a squint down the Puffing Holes from time to time. It was Tailor's spell on duty the night the whalers arrived. It was a black night – "

"'Twas all that," said the tailor eagerly, "and they carried no lights on their boat. They had found the *San Sebastian* and were climbing aboard before I heard them. They're as wily as rats."

"So Tailor came running down and he knocked us all up," said Joe Fahy.

"There were twelve of us altogether," said Ned Donnelly.

"That included myself and Michael Daly," said Bartley.

"The letter you dropped was handed in to him, and he came out to Farran at once. He was spending the night in my house."

"Mr Daly!" I exclaimed. "He was the man in glasses with the black suit, then."

"How did you know that?" asked Bartley curiously.

"Juan mentioned him specially," I said. "His men said that he was the fiercest of you all, and that he wanted you to get out the currachs and chase the trawler out to sea."

"Mr Daly enjoyed himself," said the tailor. "He said he hadn't had such a fine time since he was a boy. He wanted us to wreck the trawler and capture the whalers and trot them into Galway to the Guards' barracks in the morning."

"But we were glad enough to be able to put the run on them," said Bartley, "so long as they did no harm to the brig. We were afraid, too, that if they didn't go back to whoever had sent them, that some harm would come to you, if that had not happened already."

Then I told them how I was to have been ransomed with the *San Sebastian,* and how we had escaped up the mountain and been protected by Martin Mór, and had ridden all the way home on a horse provided by him. Just as I finished, there was a soft whinny at the door. We looked up, and saw that the horse had come around and poked his head in, and seemed to be looking meaningly at our cups of tea.

"'Tis true for you, boy!" said Mrs Folan heartily. "Come along now and I'll give you your due."

Suddenly she caught sight of the worn-out duffle-shoes.

"Glory be to goodness!" she said solemnly. "Is it making a fool of the honest beast ye were, to put that get-up on him?"

I explained how we had tried to pass silently through Cong, while I prayed that she would not see that the duffle-shoes were made of my good jersey. I was relieved when she said no more, but led the horse outside to feed him and bed him down with Bartley's pony, where no doubt they exchanged stories about their adventures for the rest of the morning.

"Perhaps the whalers won't come at all now that they can't buy the brig with Pat," said Joe Fahy, and I could have sworn that he sounded disappointed.

"They are determined to have her," I said. "Brian tells me that they think she is carrying a cargo of gold. We know her hold is empty, but every man of them is willing to risk his life to get possession of that brig."

The men looked at each other, and then they all stood up. Ned Donnelly said quietly:

"In that case we'd best be getting on with the job we were at."

"Why are you all here at this hour of the morning?" I asked suddenly.

Bartley explained that the *San Sebastian* was no longer safe in the cave, on account of the storm.

"We were going to take her around to Farran quay this morning," he said. "It will be easier to keep an eye on her there. The whalers won't be able to board her without half the population of Farran seeing them. And she'll be nice and sheltered there from the storm."

I wanted to ask:

"What about our salvage rights?"

But it seemed an ungracious question in the presence of our so willing helpers. As if he knew what was in my mind, Bartley said:

"Mr Daly says he'll see to the legal side of the

business, and he has been working at tracing her owner for the last few days."

"Has Mr Daly gone back to Galway?"

"He's up on top of the cliffs this minute," said Bartley, "watching out for the whalers. We didn't want him to go, but he insisted on taking his turn."

"He's a great man in a fight," said Lazy Johnny O'Neill.

"He's surely that," said all the men as they moved towards the door.

Outside the door everyone paused. The wind was tearing in from the west, whistling round the house, taking the words out of our mouths and tossing them high into the air. The sea was a wrinkled leaden grey. I learned that the men had brought their currachs to the beach below us, where they were now lined up waiting. We could not see the beach from where we stood, but we could hear the heavy waves rolling in, and the long drag of them on the stones as they receded.

"It's not going to be an easy job moving the brig," said Brian. "The storm is getting worse instead of better."

"But she'll have to be moved," said Bartley. "I don't like the look of that sky."

"Now, men! No time to waste!" said Joe Fahy. He led the way down to the beach, followed by all the men. Mrs Folan came too, though of course she would have to be content with watching the business from the shore.

As Brian and I followed, I looked back and saw Mr Daly running down from the cliffs towards us. He looked strangely out of place in his black clothes and his rimless spectacles. His usually careful white hair was blown upright by the wind, and he waved his arms to us as he ran, and shouted to us to wait for him.

"Ha! Trying to go without me!" he called when he was near enough. "And there is Pat home again from nowhere, and a friend with him, and no one thinks of telling me. There's gratitude!"

I felt ashamed for a moment, until I saw how Bartley laid a soothing hand on Mr Daly's arm and said:

"Ah, now Michael, it would be better for you to stay ashore. You have no experience of boats – "

"And I never will, if you have your way," said Mr Daly pettishly. "I'm not going to be left out of this. You're going to tow the brig around to the quay, aren't you? Well, I'm going, that's all! Come along, now, and no more delay!"

And he headed the procession down to the shore. The men looked at each other and shrugged, and I could see that they had intended to slip off without the lawyer and do the work in their own way. I soon understood why they had planned such an apparently ungracious course.

Launching the currachs was a task requiring a great deal of skill. With a heavy sea running, the crew of each currach had to carry the boat until they were knee-high in the water, launch it suddenly and leap aboard, snatch the oars and row outside the line of breakers in a matter of second. Mr Daly went in Bartley's currach. He ran splashingly into the sea, obviously delighting in his soaked clothes. He jumped so violently aboard that he nearly swamped us all, and he grabbed an oar and rowed vigorously in the wrong direction, until Bartley persuaded him to retire to the stern and give orders. He lay back there looking blissfully happy while Bartley and Brian and I managed the boat. When the other currachs came up on the wave-tops, I saw the men looking anxiously towards us, to see that we were safe.

It was not until we were actually at sea that I realised the full force of the storm. Rowing to the cave was very laborious, because both the tide and the wind were against us. But this would be to our advantage on the way back, when we would be steering the brig to safety. Bartley had worked out the most suitable state of tide and wind for this purpose, as he explained to us now. By the time we had arrived opposite the cave, even Mr Daly seemed impressed at the power of the elements. Bartley called a warning to him:

"Sit tight, there, Michael, till I tell you. No standing up, nor tricks of any sort!"

Though he grumbled a little, Mr Daly seemed glad to obey.

It was quieter in the lee of the cliff, though I could hear the waves thunder in the cave. We waited until the flock of currachs was around us, and then we took our currach into the cave. Brian's eyes widened with astonishment when he saw the brig. It was arranged that he and I and Mr Daly should go aboard her, and help to steer her as much as would be necessary, while the currachs would take tow-lines. Mr Daly was glad to be a member of this important party, but I saw Bartley heave a sigh of relief as he watched him climb the rope ladder and disappear over the rail. Brian and I followed in a flash, for the uneasy swell was grinding the brig on the cave walls in a way that I did not like.

Bartley cast loose the mooring-ropes and I hauled them in. Then he slipped outside again, and we threw him first one rope and then another, and another. The men's faces were set and grim, and for the first time it crossed my mind that we could fail to get the brig safely to Farran. It was always a delight to watch the team-work of these neighbours of mine, when they were at grips with the heartless sea. But the air of desperation about them now made my heart sink, as I stood at the wheel and tried to make their task easier.

At last they hauled the brig out of the cave. She rode in the lee of the cliffs for a while, until they got her head around and faced her for the open sea. There was a panic for a moment as she cleared the cliff face by inches, and then she was off, lurching under my inexpert handling, but happy enough to be towed to safety under bare poles.

Brian stood with me at the wheel, speechless with excitement as I was myself. Mr Daly was somewhere in the bows, shouting directions, mostly unnecessary, to the men. We could not see him, for the deck-houses were between us, but we could hear his voice now and then in a lull of the wind.

Then the *San Sebastian* began to roll, as she sailed out of the shelter of the cliffs. I felt the wind catch her, and she gathered speed. Soon she would be moving faster than the currachs could tow her. I had not thought of this, and I did not feel at all capable of taking the brig into the little harbour with only Mr Daly and Brian to advise me. Mr Daly knew nothing whatever about boats. I was well accustomed to handling our hookers, but the feel of the brig was quite different. I felt that it was she and not I that was master.

At this point in my reflections, the brig heeled over so that her lee rail was nearly under. I wrenched at the wheel in a panic, to find it quietly taken out of my hands by Brian.

"Let me do it, Pat," he said. "I've gone cod-fishing off the coast of Brittany in boats very like this. I know how to handle her."

This was the truth. She behaved perfectly in his hands so that I was glad to leave her to him while I went forward to see how the currachs were faring. They were in the act of casting off their tow-lines, for the brig was now out-sailing them, as I had guessed she would. Now the currachs began to fall behind, but Bartley got his in close under us. Then, while I watched, he leaped for the rope ladder and swarmed aboard the brig, leaving his currach to drift. Ned Donnelly shot across and took it in tow. As I ran to help Bartley aboard, I wondered if I would be capable of the feat he had just performed, when I would be sixty.

"I see Brian has the helm," said Bartley. "A likely boy with a boat, that lad. 'Twould do you good to study him, Pat."

"I'll have plenty of time for that," I said. "He's going to stay with me altogether."

"Good, good," said Bartley, and I knew that it was settled.

At that moment there was a wild shout from Mr Daly, still out of sight somewhere in the bows. Now he came running down the deck towards us, waving his arms and shouting, taking no heed of where he stepped, so that I thought a roll of the brig would send him overboard. But as soon as he came near enough for us to hear what he was saying, it was I who nearly fell overboard.

"The trawler!" he panted. "That one that was here before! It's there!"

"Where?" said Bartley sharply.

Mr Daly gulped and pointed seaward.

"There!" he said. "Coming after us. A crowd of men on her deck!"

We ran to the starboard rail to look. There she was, my old friend, *Santa Teresa*, forty yards away, spurting angry smoke and eating up the space between us minute by minute. She was pitching horribly in the now mountainous seas, but on her deck I could see the little group of men standing motionless, waiting only for the chance to fight for, and win, the *San Sebastian*.

13

The Battle

"How many men are there?"

"Are they armed?"

I answered Mr Daly's question first.

"There were about ten men between the two trawlers. I see five on this one, but there must be more below."

"And the arms?" said Bartley again.

"Whaling knives, knives of all kinds, polished up in our honour. I saw at least one gun – an old-fashioned pistol of some sort. They may have more."

"I'm going to heave-to," said Bartley. "We can't race them to the quay. Signal to the men to come aboard,."

He ran towards the wheel, while I stood at the port rail and waved to the men in the currachs. They had already seen the trawler, and two currachs were rowing wildly in their efforts to catch up with the *San Sebastian*. The three other currachs were making for the shore. Bartley hove-to, and I heard the anchor-chain rattle out. The brig rode there like a gull with folded wings. A minute later the first man, Ned Donnelly, clambered on board. I looked over the lee rail and saw two currachs there, busily tying up to the rope ladder.

"There will be a bit of crossness, I'm thinking," said Ned to me with a twinkle in his eye.

Joe Fahy went over and waved genially to the men on the trawler. We could hear its engine plainly now, above the storm. My heart swelled with rage and pride at the size of the task before us, but there was no time to think of that. Mr Daly was calling to me from the galley, where he had found a number of cooking-knives of various kinds. I distributed these to the men, who did not seem to like them much.

They were still grumbling among themselves when Mr Daly came forward to address them all.

"Now, men! How many are we?"

"Five and a half, Mr Daly, and two boys!" piped up little Joe Fahy.

"Five and a *half?*"

"That's right," said Joe. "There's Bartley and yourself, that's two. And Ned and Johnny and myself is five. And the tailor, of course, is half a man," he added carelessly.

There was a howl of rage from the tailor, and a howl of laughter from the others.

"But where are the rest of the men?" asked Mr Daly. "There were six currachs at the cave, and now there are only three."

212

I said, trying not to sound bewildered:

"They were rowing for the shore when I signalled to them, and I suppose they didn't understand that I wanted them to come aboard."

"Perhaps they hadn't seen the trawler," said Brian.

"Is it Mick Mahoney and Colm Hanlon and – and all the rest of them?" said Bartley in astonishment. "It couldn't be that they didn't see the trawler." He shook his head. "If Mick and Colm and all the others ran from a fight, it must be the first time in the history of Farran that such a thing happened. I can't understand it."

"Well, we must just do the best we can by ourselves," said Mr Daly cheerfully, but we could see that he was worried.

He seemed to have selected himself as general, and no one thought of disagreeing with his plan. We were to stay on deck, he said, using the deck-houses for cover. No one must go below, for fear of being cornered alone out of reach of help. Each of us was to mark one man and account for him as best he could, at the same time keeping an eye open to assist anyone who might be in difficulties. Our aim should be to disable our enemies rather than to kill them, for, said Mr Daly, we must keep on the right side of the law. We could heave them over the side into the water, however, if we wished, because then they would have a chance of swimming back to the *Santa Teresa*.

"And now, Brian," he finished, "over the side and hand up the oars of the currachs!"

There were two pairs of oars in each currach and within a minute they were lying on the heaving deck at our feet. Even as they were, they would have made fine weapons, but when Mr Daly had got each man to tie a knife to the blade of an oar, we looked like an old-fashioned army of pikemen ready to march into battle. The men were pleased with these weapons. As the tailor summed it up:

"It's nice to be able to get in a prod at your man before he gets too near, especially if you're not very well used to fighting."

"The main danger is that a man might run in under the oar," Mr Daly pointed out. "Everyone must have a knife held short in his left hand."

He was a born general, sure enough, and I could see now why Erik had such respect for him. Next, he disposed us in strategic places on the deck. It was hard to keep our footing now, for the wind had increased in force and the brig rolled and tossed alarmingly. I thought that this might be an advantage to us, if we made proper use of it. For myself, I determined to watch and attack when her bows pitched high, so that I would be poised in the air above my enemy. Waiting there behind the little galley, I felt a queer hollowness within me. I dared not begin to wonder how the brig would weather the storm.

I peeped out from my cover to see what the *Santa*

Teresa was doing, for I wondered how her crew intended to board the brig. The trawler seemed to be riding at anchor like ourselves, and her decks were deserted. Then I stepped out into the open and stared. A lifeboat with six men was pulling towards us over the crazy sea. Sometimes it disappeared into the valley between two huge waves, and then it rode aloft on the next wave as if it had risen by magic from the depths of the sea. It amazed me that they had put out in a small boat in such a storm. And still it would have been dangerous to have attempted to bring the trawler alongside the brig.

While I stood there with my mouth open, I heard a little explosion. Something smacked into the deckhouse behind my ear. I looked stupidly from the bullet to the lifeboat. Then I saw Juan, in the stern, lift his arm and take aim again. I waited for no more, but dodged to shelter again with my heart in my mouth.

Farther along the deck I could see Ned crouched, holding his oar at the ready. The tailor and Johnny O'Neill were watching for the lifeboat to come on the lee side of us, for they were sure the whalers would try to board us from there. Brian crept along behind them, and all three waited there at the top of the rope ladder prepared to make it hot for the first man whose head appeared. They could not haul up the rope ladder, for the currachs were tied to its foot.

It seemed to me that we should all assemble at the same place, for if we could keep the whalers off the

215

brig there need be no fight at all. I began to edge forward to join the others.

I do not like to think of what would have become of us without the landsman, Mr Daly. At that moment he came charging down the deck, uttering wild shouts, waving his arms and abusing us all for having left our stations.

"They've come over the stern, you louts, while you watched the ladder! After them! Charge!"

And he galloped off towards the stern. We followed in a pack, yelling lustily, as if we had not disgraced ourselves a moment ago. Even as we ran I found time to tell myself that I should have known Juan better. He was not the man to row tamely around the brig looking for a waiting ladder. He had hooked a rope over the stern rail and he and his men had swarmed aboard like rats in the twinkling of an eye.

Now began a strange game of hide and seek on the deck. There was no open fighting. We did not wish for it, and after the whalers had seen our knife-tipped oars, they did not seem to want it either. It seemed that they aimed to pick us off one by one, carefully, taking their time, and retreat with their prize, certain that they would not be followed. I saw Erik and Juan, stalking like tigers, and Manuel, trying to imitate them. There were three others who had been at the island, but I did not see the Captain at all. Later I guessed that the was waiting on his beloved *Santa Teresa*, prickling with fear for her safety.

I found myself back in my own place behind the galley with Brian, white-faced, and with a savage light in his eye. The wind had knocked the breath out of us, so that we could not speak for a moment. Then Brian panted:

"Erik is after me. I poked at him from the back with my spear. Then I had to run. He's prowling about looking for me."

At that moment, as if by magic, Erik's blond head popped around the corner of the galley. His yellow eyes shone like little lamps. He drew back his lips in a kind of silent snarl, and his bared teeth looked as big as tombstones. He began to pad purposefully towards us, while we stood fascinated, waiting for him. A cold light glinted from the blade of his upraised knife.

Suddenly I came to myself. With a shout to Brian, I ducked forward under Erik's arm. He turned to make a stab at me. Then Brian had him on the other side. Slipping and panting, we struggled with him all down the length of the deck. We had dropped our oars and now relied altogether on our strength to overcome him. I kicked his knife out of his hand the first moment we had him down. The blade glanced on my bare toe and gallons of blood, it seemed, flowed out of me. I had no time to think of it, except that it annoyed me by its slipperiness.

That was the only blood spilt. We had no wish to find out the colour of Erik's blood. He fought like a machine, but together we were more than a match for him. We got him to the stern of the brig at last, and heaved him up and over the rail, in the general direction of the lifeboat. While we rested from our labours and recovered our breath, we watched him sink and rise, and grasp the gunwale of the lifeboat while he shook the water off his face. The lifeboat plunged and rocked, but he seemed well able to hold on.

"That will keep him busy for a while," said Brian.

I almost felt sorry for him, as I looked down at the heaving green water. But there was no time to lose. As we ran back along the deck I picked up the knife still wet with my own blood. I remember wiping it carefully on my trousers before sticking it into my belt. Then as I looked up, I felt Brian clutch my arm.

Standing in front of us, six feet away, was Juan. Behind him, I could see the oars that we had dropped lying on the deck. Juan was smiling, his old charming smile that had made me trust him. It sent a shiver through me now, and all at once I felt quite helpless. I could make no move to defend myself, for apart from my sleepless night, I was exhausted from the struggle with Erik. With an effort I laid my hand on the knife in my belt. Juan said:

"Don't trouble, Pat. It will be no use."

Disgusted with myself, I dropped my hand again. In despair I wondered where all the others had gone. Where were Ned and the sailor? Where was Bartley? Perhaps they were all dead, and Brian and I were the last survivors, to be finished off in a leisurely way by the leader of the pirates himself.

But Brian was not so easily cowed. Suddenly he shot forward at full length on the deck. Stupidly I watched while he gripped Juan around the ankles. Juan swayed, but he did not fall. He began to stab at Brian. Still I could not move, until Brian shouted:

"Pat, Pat! Help me!"

I shook myself awake, and darted forward, and managed to catch Juan's hand in which the knife was raised to strike. He flocked me off, and I clutched at him again. Brian was hanging on below, trying vainly to get him down. Compared with this, the conquest of Erik had been childishly easy. With one backwards push of the elbow, Juan had me panting against the rail. Then he turned back, as he thought, to settle with Brian.

It would have gone ill with us now, but for Mr Daly. Down through the storm he came charging, waving his oar, apparently as fresh as ever he had been. And he was singing! Where he got the breath for it, I do not know, but even while he scattered Juan on the deck with one mighty sweep of his oar, his war-song trumpeted out loud and clear:

"High on the breach of Limerick with dauntless hearts they stood,
Where bombshells burst and shot fell thick and redly ran the blood!"

As he gazed down at the spreadeagled body of Juan he said anxiously:

"I've forgotten the next line of that song, Pat. Can you remember it?"

I shook my head dumbly. In a trembling voice, Brian supplied it:

"Now look you, brown-haired Moran, and mark you, swarthy Ned,

This day we'll try the thickness of many a Dutchman's head!"

"Thanks, Brian. It's been worrying me," said the lawyer. He poked at Juan. "He's only knocked out, I think. We'd better move him at once, before he has time to recover."

I suppose we were tired by now, but it seemed to me that Juan weighed as much as a young bull. It took all our strength to get him to the stern and heave him over. We took care that he should land in the lifeboat, where Erik was sitting now, green-faced.

"Catch!" called Mr Daly, as Juan crashed into the lifeboat at Erik's feet.

That boat rocked from side to side, and shipped a good deal of water, but it was not swamped, as I had feared it would be.

I looked across at the trawler, and saw that she was getting up steam, and I wondered if the Captain were going to betray his friends. Then I looked shorewards and stared, speechless, at what I saw. I could only shake Mr Daly and Brian, and point. Then we all ran forward, shouting. Now for the first time I saw Bartley and Ned and the others. They were all running too and the tailor was clutching a blood-soaked shoulder. No one else seemed to be injured. Three of the enemy followed our men. I could see that they had a brief moment of triumph, while they thought they had routed us. Then, with shrieks of fear they tumbled to the stern and threw themselves over the rail, slid down their rope and into the lifeboat.

Out from Farran, an armada of currachs was bearing down on the brig. They topped the waves and weathered the heavy seas quite unconcerned, it seemed. Three men manned each currach, and I counted fifteen currachs of them.

"There's Mick and Colm!" Bartley was pointing excitedly. "I knew they weren't running away. Good man, Mick! We were lost only for them."

"Hum," said Mr Daly.

Bartley stared at him.

"What's the matter with you, man?" he demanded.

"They spoiled our fight on us, just when it was getting lively," said Mr Daly disconsolately.

"That's true for you, Mr Daly!" said Joe Fahy at his elbow. "Sure, there's no glory in forty men getting the better of six or seven!"

"Down with you into the lifeboat, so!" said the tailor. "You can go on with the fight there."

Joe looked frightened for a moment, and then he said triumphantly:

"I can't! They've cast off!"

We turned to look. They had not waited to cast off, but had sawn hurriedly through their rope with a knife. Juan seemed to be still unconcscious, and Erik was little better. The other three were scrabbling for the oars and getting in each other's way, while their shouts rose above the wind like seagulls' cries.

Three men! I stared again. Where was Manuel? He was not in the lifeboat, which was flung away from us now and was already invisible among the tearing green waves.

But now I felt Bartley's hand on my arm and his voice in my ear quietly saying:

"The saints be praised, Pat! Look at that!"

What I saw put all other thoughts out of my head. In from the Atlantic was coming a wave the like of which I had never seen before, and hope never to see again. When I saw it, it was between us and the *Santa Teresa*. I had to tilt my head backwards to see the top of it, for it was taller than the main-mast of the *San Sebastián*. Now the others had seen it too, and were running for cover. Bartley and I followed. I had time to observe that the currachs were racing for the shore. I could see neither the *Santa Teresa* nor its lifeboat, and there was not time for more than a passing thought for them in the horror of that huge rolling monstrous wave.

Now the brig began to buck and plunge, as if there were an earthquake under her. A moment later she was clipping towards the shore before the wave, as if in some terrible race. She had broken her anchor-chain.

At the time this seemed disastrous, but later I

thought that it was the reason why we were saved. We waited momently for the wave to crash aboard us, smashing the old wooden brig to matchwood. But the *San Sebastian* had been built for such hazards, and she rode along almost as if she were enjoying herself. Closer and closer came the wave, and faster and faster she rode before it, until the shingly shore below my house was only a few yards away. Then in shallow water, inevitably she wavered. We threw ourselves on the deck, and I gave myself up for lost. The giant wave was breaking, and was lifting the *San Sebastian* on its fearful height, lifting it, running with it like an athlete with a ball, until with a tremendous crash and a thundering roar of rolling stones it tossed the brig bodily on to the beach.

Bewildered, we crawled out of the cabins where we had sheltered. The decks were still awash. There she lay, my beautiful brig, on her side high above the water-line. Seaward, we could see the murderous wave tearing off again. There was no sign of the trawler.

The beach was in ruin, with a great channel ploughed through it by the sea, and the familiar rocks whose position I had always known, tossed about like marbles. The currachs were our first concern. Bartley, looking very shaken, dropped to the ground and went across to the little group of men who were clustered around the wreckage of their precious boats. I followed him, and Ned and Johnny and the others came one by one, not knowing what fearful news would be in store for us. But the men were all safe.

"I don't know how we're all alive," said Colm Hanlon. "In all my days I never did see the beat of that wave. But we're all safe and sound."

"Are you sure? Did you count?"

"I am sure," said Colm quietly. "We're all here. But there's hardly a whole boat in the parish of Farran after this day's work. And that's a terrible misfortune."

"'Tis a terrible misfortune, a terrible disaster," said all the men.

I felt mortally ashamed. Not one of them blamed me, though it was to save the *San Sebastian* for me that they now saw their most precious possessions in ruins. Well I knew how ill they could afford to lose their boats, and how long it would be before they would be able to put together the price of building new ones.

Colm saw my despondent look. He clapped me cheerfully on the shoulder.

"Well, Pat, we made a gallant fight for the brig, and it's no one's fault that she isn't sailing into Farran quay this minute. Come over, men, till we have a look at her!"

It was never their custom to lament over misfortune, and they all came over to look at the San Sebastian, where she lay like a stranded whale.

"I doubt if she'll ever float again," said Bartley. "It would be a mighty costly business to get her repaired."

"Aye, and to build a slip to launch her," said Ned.

Mr Daly walked around to the other side of her.

"There's a disappointed man," said the tailor, as he watched his stooped shoulders and bent head.

We all stared when he came in sight again. He was completely transformed. He seemed actually to jump in his skin, as the saying is. The lazy sun sent out a thin ray that made his glasses shine. He stood there for a moment crooking his finger at us, and something of his excitement flowed into me. I clutched Brian's hand and dragged him with me. The others followed at a run.

"Something for you to see," gasped Mr Daly, and to my astonishment he burst out laughing.

He pointed to the huge gaping hole in the bows of the brig. I looked, and stood unable to move or speak, still clutching Brian's hand.

Streaming from the brig's side, like meal from a torn sack, was a cascade of gold pieces, big round gold pieces like the ones that Manuel had offered to me. And lying across them, plainly to be seen, was the skeleton of a man.

14

The End of the Story

"So that is the secret of the *San Sebastian,*" said Bartley softly at last. "And there is her cargo."

"The poor man!" said Ned. "I'd rather lie in holy ground in Farran graveyard than on a mountain of gold."

"Aye," said all the men. "Peace to his soul, whoever he was."

Mr Daly bent down to pick up one of the gold pieces. Then, holding it in his hand, he paused and said:

"Listen!"

We all heard it then, a quiet tap-tap-tap, like a tired woodpecker. Little Joe Fahy went white, and edged behind me.

"It's the ghost of the bony man, there!" he squeaked.

"That's no ghost," said Mr Daly decisively.

He clambered up the still trailing rope ladder and

disappeared over the rail. Brian and I followed him, climbing along the sloping deck with difficulty.

"He's gone down into the hold," I said. "Come on!"

Mr Daly had got the cover off the big hatch that led to the hold, and we could hear him clatter down the companion ladder. We swung down after him and dropped on to the deck below, into the half-darkness. We could dimly see Mr Daly making his shadowy way along towards a little pool of light that showed at the farthest end of the hold. And down there with the light we could hear again the tapping sound, somewhat louder now.

"What is it?" Brian whispered into my ear.

"I don't know. Someone is holding a candle."

We moved forward after Mr Daly, who had come to a halt near the light. Then I heard him say gently:

"Are you looking for something?"

I knew the face that looked up into his, but it had changed. There was still the brown skin and the shiny black hair, and the liquid brown eyes. But the eyes had a strange light in them now, like a man who has been away with the fairies. It was Manuel Carrera, of course, and what little senses he had ever had seemed to have left him.

He was crouched on the deck peering up at us, still holding the candle in one hand and in the other the stone with which he had been tapping.

"I want to open the little door," he explained slyly. "I opened it once. I just tapped and – click! It

227

opened. But now I've tapped and tapped all over, and it won't open at all!"

"Why do you want to open it, Manuel?" I asked.

"My great-great-grand-uncle is in there," Manuel said. "He went in there once – on business." he smiled at us cutely. "And the lock must have stuck, because he couldn't get out. That was a long time ago. I think he must have died in there." Two big tears gathered in his eyes. "It was terrible for him. And terrible for me in the storm. It whistled all round me, until I had to leave the brig and take to the lifeboat. The lifeboat."

He lapsed into silence. Mr Daly said:

"If you come along with us, Manuel, we can attend to your great-great-grand-uncle later. Wouldn't you like to sleep now?"

"Sleep. Yes. I would like that. And I will leave a guard here to look after the gold." It was the first time he had mentioned it. He snapped his fingers at me. "Here, you boy! Stand here without moving until I come back! Let no one in." He peered into my face, looking puzzled. "You were good to me once, I think. Yes, sleep. I am so tired."

Mr Daly got him to his feet and led him away. Brian had shrunk back into the shadows, and he came forward as soon as Manuel was gone.

"It's easy to guess at the story now," he said. "Manuel must have found the gold when he stole the brig from Juan. If that is really his great-great-grand-uncle in there," he tapped the hull with his fingers, "I should call them an unlucky family."

228

"Unlucky, sure enough," I said. "You have found the spring!"

A little door had swung towards us, and a shaft of light from the broken hull fell across our feet. We saw the gold gleam, and heard the voices of the men outside on the strand.

"Poor Manuel!" I said. "He tapped all over, searching for that lock, and you got it at one touch."

We could have gone through the little door and climbed out over the heap of gold past the skeleton of Mr Carrera, but somehow we did not want to do that. We waited until we heard Manuel move off with Michael Daly, who was taking him up to Bartley's house. Mrs Folan would look after him until he could be taken into hospital in Galway. I was not sorry that she would have something to keep her busy, so that she would not be able to come down to the shore and lament over the wreck of the *San Sebastian*.

When we came out on to the deck, we found that some of the men had gone for a horse and cart to take the skeleton away to the church. Afterwards another horse and cart was loaded with the gold, which was brought to my house. Later in the day, two astonished men came from Mr Daly's bank and brought it all into Galway. But neither Brian nor I saw any of this, for we were sound asleep in the tailor's house until nightfall.

We were roused by the tailor himself.

"Up ye get, lazybones!" he called. "Mr Daly is back from Galway, and he's over in Bartley's house. We're all going over to hear the news."

We shot out of bed.

"Why didn't you call us long ago, Tailor?" I asked reproachfully. "We've missed all the fun."

"Sure, ye were dead to the world, boy," said the tailor. "It would have been cruelty to rouse ye. And anyway, 'twas only the work ye missed. The fun will come now, over in Bartley's."

We lost no time in getting to Bartley's house, and on the way we made the tailor tell us the news of the day. Manuel had gone into Galway with Mr Daly, and everyone hoped that he would have told his part of the story to the lawyer by now. The brig still lay where we had left her, but she was well above the normal high-water-mark. The men agreed that it was unlikely that there would be any more bad storms before the autumn, but for extra safety they had spent the afternoon in building a breakwater of stones to protect her.

"How many of the currachs are seaworthy now?" I asked, just as we reached Bartley's door.

"Two," said the tailor.

An idea was growing in my mind, but it was not yet complete enough to be mentioned. The tailor looked at me sharply, but he asked no questions.

In Bartley's kitchen, Mr Daly had the place of honour on the hob. Bartley sat on the other hob, and Mrs Folan, unable to sit still with excitement, trotted in and out among the people on a series of unnecessary errands.

"I thought you were going to sleep round the

clock, Pat," she said when she caught sight of me. "Mr Daly couldn't begin to tell his story until you arrived."

She made me and Brian come and sit at the table, where we drank tea and ate soda-bread while Mr Daly talked. The men were already toasting the *San Sebastian* in whiskey. Joe Fahy had buttermilk in his.

"It will take time to get the whole story," the lawyer began. "Manuel has told me a great deal of it, but he is not a clever man, and he doesn't really know much of the history of Chile."

"Then all that part about Chile was true!" I exclaimed.

"Some of it was true," said Mr. Daly. "Manuel told you that the *San Sebastian* was built in Valparaiso in 1819. That was true, as the papers that Mrs Folan has will prove. I do not know if Manuel's other name is Carrera, but I do know that he is not the great-great-grand-nephew of Juan José Carrera, the Chilean General-in-Chief. He is the descendant of the General's batman, whose skeleton we found in the hull of the brig.

"It is a strange and complicated story. At the time of the revolution, as often happens, people were afraid to put their money in the banks. It seems that a great deal of money was entrusted to the General, perhaps to keep in safety until the end of the fighting, but possibly to buy arms for his men. As Manuel said, General Carrera was defeated at first, but he raised a new army in Buenos Aires and came back to win the battle of Chacabuco. That was in 1817, and two years later the General's batman is strangely rich enough to have the San Sebastian built, and to sail away on her to Spain. It was no one's business to prevent him, it seems, though he made no secret of his intention to go to the enemy country. Perhaps confusion was caused by the fact that the Chileans had gone to help Peru in her war of independence. I think it is obvious that the batman stole the money somehow, but it will be difficult to find that part of the story."

"Where does Juan come in?" asked Brian.

"Here again we can only guess," said Mr Daly. "He told Pat that he was the descendant of Mateo de Toro, the Governor of Chile, but Manuel says that that is a lie. Manuel says that Juan's mother was a descendant of the carpenter who built the secret bulkhead in the hull of the *San Sebastian*.

"That sounds more like the truth," Bartley nodded.

"Now we come to the history of the brig when she reached Spain," Mr Daly went on. "The General's batman sailed to Santander, where he was welcomed with open arms as a Spanish gentleman fleeing from the Chilean revolution. He had a crew of Spanish sailors who had been stranded in Chile, and whom he paid off in Santander. He also had on board the carpenter who had built the storage place for the gold. This man had been paid in gold, but he had also bargained that he was to be brought back to Spain in the *San Sebastian*. He set up in business as a timber merchant in a neighbouring town."

"The batman anchored his brig in the harbour and went ashore. He bought fine clothes, and a carriage and horses, and made friends with all the wealthy people in the town. He did not dare to bring his gold ashore until the excitement of the revolution would have died down. The next thing that happened was that he married an heiress, the daughter of a big ship-owner in Santander. He went into partnership with his wife's father, and within a year he had become one of the most respected citizens of the town. The *San Sebastian* remained at anchor in the harbour, as a sort of advertisement for the shipping company."

"So she really made only one voyage in her life," I said.

"Yes. She never went to sea again. About a year after his marriage, the batman – whose name I don't know yet – went out one night and never returned. We can imagine how his wife and her father started a search for him, how they hoped from day to day that he would come back. And all the time he was on board his own brig, shut into the secret compartment. We do not know how this happened. He had rowed out there to count his money and gloat over it, as he did from time to time. Perhaps the lock stuck and he could not open it, or perhaps he got a seizure of some kind and died. In any case, his family never thought to look for him there, and there he stayed with his secret gold."

"And sure, 'twas no use to him then," said the tailor, shaking his head.

"After that, no one thought of putting to sea in the brig again. It was not known whether her owner was alive or dead, and I suppose that as long as it seemed possible that he might return home, it was thought better to keep his property in good order. The *San Sebastian* was kept painted and polished, and in a state of good repair, and all her furnishings exactly as they were originally, so that she remained always as seaworthy as the day she sailed from Valparaiso. Long after her owner would have died of old age, if he had not died otherwise, she was tended like a baby, until it was a tradition in the company that no one would have thought of breaking.

"Meanwhile, as I said, the carpenter had set up in business as a timber merchant in a neighbouring town. He seems to have been a shiftless person and he never really made good. He dragged along for a while, made a little money and lost it again, and at last went bankrupt. Then he moved his family to Santander, where he did odd jobs on ships in port. No doubt the sight of the San Sebastian at anchor before his eyes annoyed him, but he was afraid of her owner, and he did not tell his secret until he was dying. Then he told his wife, but she thought he was romancing and she took no notice. She remembered it later on, however, and told her son, but he was a poor honest man who did not want to get into trouble, and he did nothing either. Still, the story passed from father to son that there was a huge cache of gold on the *San Sebastian,* until it came to Juan's turn to hear about it.

"Juan is a descendant of the carpenter, Manuel says. he was already the leader of a little band of water-thieves with agents in many countries, when he heard the story."

"I suppose the Janviers in that town in Brittany were his agents," I said, and added: "I wonder what was the name of that town?"

"Manuel may tell us," said Mr Daly. "Yes, the Janviers were agents of Juan's. Little trawlers could put in at any of the ports where his friends were, without attracting attention. They used to steal cargo piled up on the quays waiting to be shipped, and go off with it quietly and sell it somewhere else. But stealing the *San Sebastian* was the boldest thing they had ever planned."

"Manuel was at Santander making all the arrangements. The *Santa Teresa* and the *San Fernando* were fishing quietly outside the bay. They slipped in one night and freed the brig, and sailed her out without any trouble. They took her up the coast to a lonely little bay, where they kept her for a few days while they made plans to sail her to the Canary Islands. It was then that they took the trouble to remove the labels from the blankets to make it harder to trace the ownership of the brig. They were delighted with her – they are a romantic enough lot, for all their black hearts."

"It was there that she got so dirty, I suppose," I said aside to Bartley.

"Manuel watched his chance," Mr Daly went on, "until he found himself one night alone on the brig. He thought he knew how to handle her by himself now, and of course he did not scruple to deceive his confederates. He thought he would take her to England and abandon her, having first removed the gold. Even in fair weather it is doubtful if he could have managed her, but as it happened a storm got up, and he was helpless. Juan followed him in the *Santa Teresa* for a good piece of the way, for they missed him quite soon. He was blown to the Irish coast at last, and in the most violent part of the storm, they lost him.

"We know the rest of the story – how Pat found him in the lifeboat, and brought him home, and how Juan from his hiding-place in Henry's Cove directed Pat's capture and took him away to Brittany."

"Why did they ransack my house?" I wanted to know.

"For the ship's papers, to be sure. They were not content to have the gold. They also wanted to sell the brig to some unsuspecting person, and they could not do this without the papers. They guessed, of course, that Pat would have removed the papers from the brig at the first possible moment."

"'Twas no wonder the *San Sebastian* was wrecked," said Ned Donnelly. "How could she have luck and the skeleton of a man sailing everywhere in her? Wouldn't you think, now, that they'd have taken him out and buried him decent somewhere? Aren't they the hard-hearted lot!"

"As far as I know, they had never seen the skeleton," said Mr Daly. "Manuel says they had not yet found the gold at the time they stole the brig. They were in too much of a hurry to get away, and it was enough for them that the story said it was there. Manuel himself found the secret door when he was at sea, not long before the storm broke. He guessed at once whose the skeleton was. He's not very sensible today, but I understand that he found it very hard to take to the lifeboat and leave all the gold behind. So he filled his money-belt with it before he left."

"Foolish man," said Bartley. "Its weight would have been enough to sink him if the lifeboat had overturned."

Lazy Johnny O'Neill said:

"If Pat and Brian had not escaped, we would have had to hand over the brig to those pirates. They were clever enough to know that we couldn't see him come to any harm."

"Will the gold be mine now?" I asked the lawyer.

"As far as I can see, it will," he said. "Even if it were not yours by right of salvage, it would be impossible now to trace its owners. I think any court would award it to you."

"What kind of money is it?"

"Spanish dollars, not currency now, of course. It's value will be in the gold."

I asked the next question in a low voice, so that the men would not hear me. They had begun to talk it all over among themselves, and to clear up the stray ends of the story. Mr Daly leaned forward to hear me.

"Will there be enough to pay for the repairing of the brig so that she can sail again?"

"Do you want to do that?"

"More than anything in the world!"

Brian had heard too, and his eyes sparkled at this. Mr Daly said slowly;

"Yes, there will be enough to have the *San Sebastian* repaired, and a great deal more besides."

"Will there be enough to buy a little fleet of trawlers for the men of Farran to go fishing in, and to buy them wood and canvas to build more currachs?"

My voice had risen with excitement, though I did not know it. All the men were listening now. Mr Daly looked around the kitchen.

"Yes, I think there will be enough for that," he said.

And there was enough. I remember how we sat talking in Bartley's kitchen until the dawn, going over and over every detail of the adventure. In the morning Mr Daly went home to Galway, with a promise from us that he would be a member of the crew of the *San Sebastian* as soon as she would be afloat again. We knew that many a day would pass before this would come about, but we were not impatient now. There were so many plans to be made for the new fleet of trawlers that we were all kept busy. The opinions of everyone had to be sought, even of the landsmen like the tailor and the weaver and the blacksmith and Matt Faherty who owned the shop. Martin Mór came for the horse in a few days, as he had said he would, and there was all the fun of telling him the whole story all over again. He and Bartley became great friends.

Brian stayed with me, and we had as much fun together as I had imagined, and more. He was a wonderful companion, and an invaluable member of our crew when at last we had our little fleet of trawlers.

A strange thing was that Manuel decided to stay with us too. He liked Farran, he said, and the people were good to him. The men shrugged and smiled, and let him stay. He was useful for piloting us to the fishing-grounds, and he showed us a special secret way that the Spaniards have for casting a trawl net. But if ever a Spanish trawler hove in sight, Manuel would go below, and nothing would persuade him to come up until the coast was clear.

He need not have troubled. From that day to this, we never laid eyes on Juan nor on any member of his crew again. Whether the *Santa Teresa* foundered when the big wave struck her, or whether the men in the lifeboat got aboard her and sailed away, we never discovered. Though it may seem hard-hearted to some, I will be honest enough to say that we did not care.

Other Poolbeg Classics for you to enjoy!

The Sea Wall by Eilís Dillon
ISBN: 185371304X

My Friend Specs McCann by Janet McNeill
ISBN: 1853715379

The Bookshop on the Quay by Patricia Lynch
ISBN: 1853714437

Fiddler's Quest by Patricia Lynch
ISBN: 1853713333

The Grey Goose of Kilnevin by Patricia Lynch
ISBN: 1853714062

The Dark Sailor of Youghal by Patricia Lynch
ISBN: 1853715174

Beyond the Wide World's End by Meta Mayne Reid
ISBN: 1853715093

The Two Rebels by Meta Mayne Reid
ISBN: 1853713430